The Price of Passion

an erotic journey

Also by the Author:

Lip Service
Lesbians Raising Sons (ed.)
AfterShocks
Two Willow Chairs
The Dress / The Sharda Stories
The Herstory of Prostitution in Western Europe
Run

The Price of Passion

an erotic journey

by Jess Wells

Firebrand
Books
Ithaca, New York

This book may not be reproduced in whole or in part, except in the case of reviews, without permission from Firebrand Books, 141 The Commons, Ithaca, New York 14850.

Book design by Sunset Design
Cover design by Look At That
Cover photograph by Yael Daphna Saar

Printed in the U.S. by McNaughton & Gunn

10 9 8 7 6 5 4 3 2 1

Library of Congress Cataloging-in-Publication Data

Wells, Jess
    The price of passion : an erotic journey / by Jess Wells.
      p. cm.
    ISBN 1–56341–113–X (alk. paper)—ISBN 1–56341–112–1
      (pbk. : alk.paper)
    I. Title.
PS3573.E488 P75 1999
813'.54—dc21
                                                    99–047445

Simone regarded the rippled side of the oily train as if it were the face of a loved one. It was finished now, her incredible journey toward lust and connection, a lifetime of travel, and the sensations ran over her skin: the smell of warm arms, the press of lips against her thighs, the aroma of wet hair, the touch of silk and burlap, of cotton sheets still hanging on the line as her body was pressed into them. Whose breath was it that she could feel against the soft skin between her lip and nose? All of them. The lovers who let slip the acrid smell of calamari, the sweet of Schnapps on clean teeth, the musk of wine and nutty tobacco—all sighing against her face, their tiny breaths full of gratitude and self-absorption.

At sixty-six, she was tired; home, finally, in Boston, but more disoriented than if she had missed a connection in Zimbabwe. She swayed unsteadily as the train wrenched itself from the station, gathering speed, tearing her past away from her and leaving her coated with a cindery dust and the stench of diesel. Simone turned, caught by a glimpse of her name scrawled on a placard. She took a step backward when she saw that the sign was being carried by a thin young woman in khakis and a white shirt, whose mane of black hair was exactly the color that hers had been when she was that age. The eyes, the nose—this woman walking toward her *was* Simone, a memory whose hair shimmered like her own forty years ago. Hair that had made people on the sidewalk lean into her to inhale the color, had made women beg to sleep all night in her tangles. This vision in the train station held Simone's placard more as a nameplate, more as an identification of *herself* than as a way to find Simone, and the old woman thought that time had finally turned back upon itself.

Through her travels, she had been looking for her past, her mother, her lineage, her purpose and place. To construct herself. Now that her journey was over, she was back to being the young woman she had been when she stepped onto a train with the name of her first destination clutched in an envelope in her hand, unawares, uninitiated, an unformed woman who would have gladly carried a sign like a breastplate if it could have made her identity real, given her a home. Simone, watching herself approach, thought that time had bent once and for all, that her mind had slipped into the vortex of her vagabond life and had whirled full circle, bringing her back to her own youth. This young woman who proffered her cardboard sign was Simone, except that this time around, Simone strained to see, the girl had full knowledge of who she was. Didn't she?

Simone's knees buckled. No, there in the young woman's eyes was the same lonely confusion Simone had displayed when she had first begun this journey. The girl's eyes, dark and bitter with neglect, would glance at but never see gestures of affection and evidence of love. Her eyes showed Simone a longing so unfulfilled that she had resigned herself to it, convinced that no tenderness could ever heal it. But the girl was wrong.

Simone had spent four decades proving her wrong. She saw the young woman moving directly toward her. If the woman was her own past cycling around to reclaim her, would Simone be sucked into the journey again, forced to battle her own maelstrom as she had from the beginning? She fell into a faint on her luggage.

*T*elegram for Simone Fitzwater!" the thin voice of the young boy had announced at the desk of the college dormitory more than forty years ago.

Simone skipped down the stairs with her brown leather rucksack and her diploma.

COME AT ONCE ANDOVER HOUSE. NANNA VERY ILL.

The maid who accompanied Simone along the narrow corridor to her grandmother's room quietly opened the door. Simone slipped into the dark, her heart pounding. Finally freed from what had always felt like exile at school, could she be about to lose the only family member she had?

She felt out of place surrounded by her grandmother's lace and tapestries, china on pedestals, tassels, Moroccan leather boxes, Asian masks, glistening Italian marble eggs. She straightened her rough cotton shirt and her thread-worn chinos, and pushed her thick hair off her face.

Simone supposed this was her ancestral home. Although she used it as her permanent address, she had only been here once before. She tried to recognize a perfume, struggled to remember whether she had ever seen her grandmother buy any of the objects around her. She imagined that the furniture had belonged to relatives, that there were stories surrounding each settee and bureau, but Simone's family history was more of a family mystery.

Her father had died without Simone forming any memories of him. Her mother was agoraphobic, refusing to leave an apartment she had kept in Boston. Groceries arrived in the arms of young boys, the dry cleaning was carried out by a service. Simone had been escorted to school, to the playground or the doctor by a series of nannies who never stayed long enough to know her. Her life with her mother had been a contained one behind drawn shades, where they nestled together on the couch like birds in a bush. Simone's grandmother had spent her time traveling the world, and Simone could barely remember instances where she, her mother, and her grandmother had been together long enough to share a turkey or open a festive box.

When Simone was ten years old, her mother had re-married, this time to an alcoholic who had banished Simone to a boarding school.

"George says we're too close," her mother had whispered as Simone listened to the sound of her stepfather's ice swirling around in his glass. "Just too close."

Her mother had cried and wrung her hands, but Simone was packed up, given a gift of the leather rucksack she still carried, and put on a train for her school several states away.

The first months of boarding school she had spent all her time out of class huddled under a blanket in her room with the shades drawn. Gradually, she had been able to join the girls for walks. When she could finally lie alone, outside, in the newly cut grass of the grounds, she had spread her arms and legs wide and cried with fear and joy, exhilarated over the freedom, the daring.

Later that year, the headmistress had called her into the office and told her that her mother and stepfather had died in a car accident. Simone had required no explanation—she knew that her stepfather had been drunk. But for years she kept wondering how he had gotten her mother out of the house. What power had he possessed that Simone did not? What had her mother felt for him that would make her don a hat, open the door?

Simone had become her grandmother's ward after the accident. She shipped the girl back to school and sent her postcards containing brief, mysterious words from exotic locales, cryptic notes from Bali that Simone would try to decipher, little half-poems from Milan or tombstone inscriptions from Paris, playbills and ticket stubs from festival towns in Italy. Young Simone had interpreted them as the whispers of spirits, angels, of her mother once removed. The women in her life were now a very long way away—her mother in heaven and her grandmother in earthly places Simone had never seen.

As the years of her childhood passed, Simone had been summoned by her grandmother to lush hotels for holidays during which her grandmother would stride across crystal-festooned lobbies, sweep up her little charge, whirl her through festivities, and then set her on a plane again. In the first minutes after her arrival Simone would nestle into her nana's arms trying to inhale her scent, remember her hair, the shape of her hands, a gesture to bring her home. She clung to her nana's hand, neither able to look upward toward the woman nor inward toward her own life because all activities were focused outward: on viewing, on seeing places, witnessing culture, observing architecture, animals, theater that went by in a jumbled kaleidoscope of colors and shapes.

And each visit Simone saw what seemed to be a different woman. Her nana was a redhead in daring slacks, then a raven-haired woman in a ball gown. Simone was whisked through strange countries, introduced to exotic friends. There was always a new spin, an enthusiasm in her nana's life that the woman embraced with devotion until it was dropped and she flew off to a new locale, a new devotion. She was passionate about duck habitats, then the opera, then Arctic fox survival, the cut of coattails in Paris. She was the vociferous, emblazoned champion of a hundred causes that she called her own, sending her granddaughter posters and brochures without letters, the good fight that she then abandoned. What she created in her wake was a small amount of social change, a large number of memories, and a granddaughter who had a very poor grasp on who her nana actually was.

Her grandmother had seemed as incapable of staying as her mother had been of leaving. Her mother had been all nest, her grandmother all flight.

Simone had traced her nana's travels as if she could overtake the messages, pin them down to a location, and, in so doing, find a place where someday she and her grandmother would be together. She had studied the cultures of her grandmother's travels in the hopes of finding a commonality, a heritage, a language, a thread.

Was this the place, Simone wondered, inhaling the fragrance of the old woman's room? Home from travels, out of school, the two might actually intersect this time. Staring at the sofa along the wall, she felt her cheek against the soft tapestry pillows, felt herself sinking into the down cushions, remembered the glorious press of her mother's body behind her, her arm across Simone's chest, lying like spoons in the stillness of their private world. A day like that had to come again. Someday. She had waited so long.

Now her nana lay sleeping in bed—white-haired, wrinkled, still—unrecognizable. Not dancing, entertaining, waving at waiters. The old woman was very pale, but she glowed as if she were melting, fine china tossed into the fire. Simone grabbed her nana's hand hungrily. Other women grew up with the surety of heritage, knowledge, affection. Simone had a vague recollection of what four inches of palm skin felt like.

"Nana," Simone whispered plaintively.

A woman touched Simone's elbow. "I'm Phyllis, your grandmother's...personal secretary." Simone was startled by how much the woman looked like a sparrow, tiny and plain as she clutched the edges of her brown woolen cardigan for courage. "I'm afraid Abigail's taken a turn for the worse," Phyllis said breathlessly, as if unaccustomed to the permission to speak. "The disease seems to be progressing much faster than we had expected."

Phyllis and Simone were startled by a commotion in the hallway. Phyllis opened the door a crack and peeked out at the chauffeur who was carting in Simone's luggage from college.

"Now, did you formulate any plans?" Phyllis asked tentatively.

Simone shook her head as if answering a deeper question. Like most college girls who had grown out of their child's body but not into a woman's life, Simone stood undecided and un-easy between two lives. And because of the polar-opposite lives of the two women who had been in her childhood, she was more undecided than most. At this moment, Simone wanted to announce herself home and never leave, pull the curtains closed, and live with the old woman.

The maid was instructed to ready one of the rooms.

That night, Simone wandered through the grand house with a glass of brandy, touching the booty from her grandmother's journeys, recognizing a few opera trinkets and carved boxes, but generally overwhelmed by the rich life that had clearly been lived without her. She was no more able to decipher who her nana was than before. As she walked down the hallway to her nana's bedroom she heard moaning, then her grandmother shout-ing. Phyllis came out of the room, her hair disheveled and her eyes frightened. She grasped Simone's elbow with a surpris-ing level of intention and guided her into the room. The old woman tried to raise herself onto the pillows.

"Tell me…about Jana," Simone's grandmother said deliri-ously. "Dancing. Tell me."

Phyllis slid into her chair next to the bed and took Abi-gail's hand, raised it to her lips, and kissed it. She made little clucking sounds and patted the old woman's hand to quiet her.

"I want to know about Jana," Abigail moaned, and Phyl-lis laid her face on Abigail's forearm. Simone was surprised by the gesture and by the way her grandmother closed her eyes, squeezing the bird-woman's hand. Such an intimate gesture of fear and trust and companionship.

Phyllis dug into the deep pockets of her cardigan and produced the nib of a pencil. She scribbled on a piece of paper, then tucked the paper into a small manila envelope. She patted Abigail's forearm in reassurance and scurried to Simone.

"Please, my dear," she implored Simone. "There is a list of people who need to know…that she is ill. She wants you to go to them, each of them."

Her grandmother struggled for breath. "Tell them I have always loved them."

Phyllis took Simone by the elbow again, gently this time, and lowered her voice. "We'll give you one hundred thousand dollars to go to Stockholm. Do you understand?"

"One hundred thousand dollars?" Simone was astounded. Money had never been discussed between them. She knew she was from a wealthy family; the house and the trips told her that. Schools had been paid for, tickets appeared, but spending money had been produced only when Simone arrived for visits or when she asked for something in particular. There had never been any money free of strings. Since there was always so little time to discuss what really mattered to Simone, she had never bothered to waste it on conversations about money. She had lived through as many bare cupboard days as other college students and not chided herself for her reticence in inquiring about her finances. The lapses in money just seemed part of the lapses in tenderness, togetherness.

"She *needs* her memories," Phyllis implored.

More than she needs me, obviously, Simone thought bitterly. Money for command performances. More hotel trips. It was an exchange she was accustomed to.

"You want me to—convey your love?" Simone called skeptically over the sparrow's shoulder to her grandmother. "Nana, do you want me to *write* to them?"

"No, no," her nana said hastily. "These are matters of the flesh, my dear. You'll understand once you're there. Paper and ink are not suitable for the conveyance."

Not suitable, Simone thought, stuffing her hands into her pockets. Paper and ink seemed to be enough to raise a child, she grumbled to herself, remembering the nights she had spent on the cold school floor pouring through her shoebox of post-cards from her grandmother. She had tried to wring some gesture of affection from them, some warmth from their locations, their gaiety. It seemed to Simone that she had been traveling since the day she walked out while her mother cried softly in the background. The boarding school, summer camp, a few junkets with her grandmother. Nine different apartments and dorm rooms in four years of college, scores of odd jobs in the summers when there was no sign of her grandmother, and now her nana was asking her to get on the road again.

"So, I go to Stockholm. Then what?" Simone asked with a surprising bitterness to her voice.

"We will send you another name," Phyllis said, wringing the edge of her cardigan, "and another installment of money." She pulled her sweater around her throat and bent close to Simone. She whispered. "There is thirteen million dollars at stake here."

"Thirteen? Good Lord!" Simone said. She had had no idea.

"I'm told it is the condition of your inheritance."

"And if I refuse?"

"Children receive," Abigail said with a rasp in her throat,

"adults earn. Time to grow up, my sweet."

"I'm so sorry," Phyllis said quietly, "but my dear, there are more than sixty-five charities worldwide carrying your grandmother's name that would be happy to receive it instead."

All right. Staying put was clearly a dangerous decision, Simone thought. Not only because of the money, but because staying would involve living here with a dying woman, living through more loss, and then being left in an empty house. Her mother had chosen the home life, and it had swallowed her up into a world without radio or television, where she had lived in fear of the doorbell, cried over the prospect of a grocery store. Curl into the suffocating and terrified closeness of her mother's choice of home, or embrace her grandmother's passionate globetrotting? At least on this trip she would have a chance to visit the old woman's life, to peek into the world Simone had longed to know, to share.

"I love you, Nana," Simone said softly.

Abigail motioned the girl forward. Simone moved to the side of the bed, sat on its edge and leaned over to kiss her grandmother. The scent of old-fashioned laundry soap rose from the sheets as she bent and pressed her lips into the woman's cheek. "I love you too, my dearest darling," Abigail whispered. "Love orchestrates its own revelation. I wish it was something I could change."

"You must leave now," Phyllis said softly, escorting Simone into the hall.

"Now? What if she dies while I'm gone?" Simone paced nervously back and forth.

"Be her eyes," Phyllis said. "Go and bring her her memories. Let her reconnect with her past through you. She needs that."

"I should have visited more often."

"Nonsense," Phyllis said. "She only arrived home to stay a few years ago herself. She wasn't much of a grandmother to you, but...she will be. Here's a portion of the first allotment for expenses. We'll send the next name to general delivery in Stockholm," Phyllis said, handing Simone the brown envelope. "Now go." She lifted the brandy snifter from Simone's hand and pointed to the leather rucksack that was still sitting by the door, her jacket that lay on top of it. "There isn't any time to lose, my dear."

Simone looked around at Abigail's memorabilia, her museum of escapades. I'll explore her memories, Simone thought, but for myself, for my own need to thread through her past.

The old woman called from the next room. "Phyllis, my darling, come and dance with me again."

Phyllis smiled and opened the door wider for Simone's departure. She called back to the bedroom, "In a heartbeat, my dearest."

*A*s the tram rattled through the crowded streets of Stockholm, Simone fingered the small envelope, a map, and a phrase book.

"Jana Stor, at 652 Strandvägen," Simone recited to herself. Perhaps a cup of tea, then on to the hotel. Nothing complicated. The woman was even in the phone book.

"Abigail Fitzwater has sent me," she said to the maid who answered the door.

"Fitzwater?" the maid interrupted and motioned her into the hall.

"My grandmother, Abigail Fitzwater, has requested that I—"

"Just a moment please." The maid hurried through an ornate living room. Rather confused at the maid's abrupt departure at the sound of her grandmother's name, Simone shifted the rucksack on her shoulder. She heard a door open and close quietly behind the maid, then open again almost immediately.

"You may see Madam Stor," the maid said. "This way." Simone ran her hand through her hair and attempted to straighten her shirt. At the large wooden door to the library, the maid reached out her hand for Simone's rucksack.

Simone cleared her throat, looked around at the high ceilings, the white sunshine that bathed the muslin curtains and pale flowered upholstery.

"Oh my God, you *are* Abigail," a husky voice said.

Simone turned. A woman stood in the corner behind an expansive desk draped in a rust-colored cloth. The dramatic pattern of the cloth and the riotous leaves of a potted plant behind her obscured her outline.

"No. Her granddaughter."

The woman turned away, covered her mouth, then turned back. "Exactly like her. Twenty years fall away just looking at you," Jana said, stepping toward Simone. Jana was tall and broad-shouldered, her white hair pinned into a French twist. "Remarkable resemblance."

"I hadn't noticed, actually. Madam, I'm sorry to just appear on your doorstep, but—"

"What a relief to have you here. Just to have some small part of Abigail again." Her gold, brown, and rust-colored dress rippled with her movement as she traversed the room and took Simone's face in her hands, startling her. The woman's blue eyes were like ice chips.

"Do you know your grandmother?" the woman asked, still holding Simone's face very close to her own.

"Not well."

"I suppose this means she's dying," the woman said softly, dropping her hands.

"I don't know if this is the proper moment, but she's sent me to tell you..." Simone looked around the room to be sure they were alone, "that she's always loved you."

The woman looked away, touched the tips of her teeth with her tongue. "My God, we're going to miss her. You will stay with me awhile, won't you?" she said very tearfully, moving closer to Simone.

"Well, I should get back to her."

"Would you like to call to check in?"

"Yes, very much so."

Phyllis was pleased Simone had arrived, and Simone heard her grandmother's chortle in the background at the news. What was Jana wearing, she wanted to know? How did she look?

"She looks…marvelous," Simone whispered into the receiver.

"She wants to know about the sauna," Phyllis said.

"The sauna?"

"Yes. She says to have a nice sauna and ask Jana about dancing."

Jana called from across the room. "You're fond of the sauna? Abigail adores the sauna. We'll go right away."

Simone stripped off her clothing in front of the second-floor balcony lockers on the women's side of the Stockholm Baths. Built on three sides of the room, the balcony was a complex of lockers and wooden benches where women slowly wove in and out, stripping panties off thighs, sauntering naked with towels over their shoulders.

Simone was tall, even among these Swedes, nearly six feet, boy-like with her taut belly and muscled thighs. She stood slightly hunched over, hiding her breasts. Disconcerted that the towel was too small to actually cover her, Simone quickly twisted the terrycloth around her hips, tossed her clothing into a locker, and headed for the stairs and the water to hide in. A tub, a bit of dinner. She wished she had the complete list so she could finish up and get back to her grandmother. Simone wanted to spend time at her bedside, hear about the places she had been, find out how her own life was destined to shape up if the old woman died. Not until the list was finished, though. She owed her nana that much, money or no money.

The steam rose from the pool, up the two stories of blue tile chipped with age, worn smooth with the steam and sweat and the smell of herbs rising from women's skin. Water poured from a fountain on the wall. Simone slowly descended into the scalding water. The pool of water expanded the outline of her skin, blurred time. Simone couldn't see the edges of the room. Women appeared from the mist, then disappeared under the surface of the water. She floated undefined on the cusp of change, her skin in the hot water asking who she was, where she was going. She gave herself up to the heat, relinquishing her clutching desire for answers, for direction, and laid back into water so fragrant that it relaxed her shoulders and consumed her hair. Abigail loves the sauna, Jana had said. She had been here, Simone thought, feeling her grandmother through her skin.

Opening her eyes, she saw Jana gingerly walking down the stairs, cradling her voluminous breasts like an armload of overly ripe fruit. Her skin was translucent white, tight over her legs and hipbones, soft and yielding over her belly. Her white hair hung like a veil down her back which was slightly stooped now that she was relieved of her proper library and big house. Jana slid into the water, her succulent breasts rising to chest level and her hands stroking through the blue water.

Simone leaned against the smooth tile wall, the fountain pounding water inches from her shoulder. Jana moved in front of her, the water making the ends of her hair heavy. She reached out and cupped Simone's wet head in her hand, drew herself near. "To have just a bit of Abigail again," the old woman said, closing her eyes and inhaling deeply.

Simone's breath came short and fast as Jana pressed her breasts into Simone and held her close.

"Now turn, my little bit of Abigail," Jana demanded, moving Simone by her shoulders, then standing aside. Simone allowed herself to be turned over to a masseuse, who positioned a hot towel against the pool's edge for Simone to lean on before she began to work on her shoulders. The woman's thighs brushed against Simone's arms, her muff against her back as she kneaded Simone's muscles. The masseuse passed her along to another naked woman waiting in the steamy water. She wrapped her arms under Simone's arms and twisted her spine. When they brought Simone out of the water and laid her on a pallet, in full view of the other patrons, she stretched out and closed her eyes, limp and willing.

Back at Jana's house, the maid walked into the room without knocking while Simone stood in her chinos, holding her bra.

"Madame says perhaps you'd like to try a few of the clothes your grandmother kept here." Without flinching, the maid handed her a soft blouse which Simone pulled to her to shield her breasts. The maid turned on her heels and left.

The maid returned with a decanter of gin and a small glass. Simone uncorked the bottle immediately as the maid closed the door behind her. Simone slipped into her bra and then tentatively into the blouse, seeing her grandmother's hands at the end of Simone's cuffs. Inhaling deeply, she took off the blouse, removed her bra to better feel the fabric, and slid into the blouse again.

The maid returned. "The guests are arriving." She held out a pair of fine black slacks. Simone was still damp from the sauna, her skin inside her clothes searching for its boundaries as if the heat had challenged her to sketch herself anew. She roughly grabbed the tongue of her belt, deftly unclasped and unzipped her own crumpled chinos, and let them drop to the floor. She and the maid locked gazes, and Simone's body flushed from the unaccustomed challenge and her own first attempt at bravado. She slid into the trousers, cinching them tightly.

"What guests?"

"Celebrants of Abigail," the maid said.

Simone smiled and poured herself another gin.

When she descended into the main parlor, three women Jana's age, each holding a long-stemmed crystal champagne glass, gasped at the sight of Simone. One bit her lip and touched her throat. *Abigail,* Simone heard. Jana strode to Simone and brought her forward. Simone felt like a specimen, and judging from the reaction on the old women's faces, a creature filled as much with her nana's personality as her own. It pleased her, though. It was exhilarating to be someone who was nearly complete, someone who belonged and had a past.

Simone let the past and the present mingle in her throat, in her chest, in the tips of her breasts, like the champagne she was handed, now sliding into her bloodstream, and the silk chafing against her nipples.

The women clutched at her hand and spoke incomprehensible Swedish with love in their eyes. They relayed stories she couldn't understand, escorted her to the buffet table, refilled her glass, and snuggled next to her on the couch. They chided each other for monopolizing her. Together, they brought her to the picture-laden mantelpiece. An old wooden frame caught Simone's eye: it contained a photograph even Simone mistook for herself. It was her grandmother standing on a small pier with her arm around a very young Jana Stor. Simone picked up another picture: Abigail and Jana lying in each other's arms on a picnic blanket, Abigail looking very butch with slicked-back hair and a white shirt. Simone picked up one of the frames and held it to her chest. Home—it was a piece of home. If she followed the envelopes she would discover the course of her grandmother's life, able to share it now even though she had been sent away as a child.

"Abigail has asked for a report on dancing," Simone said, fingering the rim of her glass. Emboldened by the champagne, she picked up Jana's hand and kissed her knuckles, then turned her hand and kissed Jana's palm, her wrist.

Jana translated with a smile, and her statement sent a flurry through the room. She picked up the phone. The older women applauded, giggled, staked out places on chaise lounges and overstuffed chairs. Removing their shoes and unbuttoning their blouses, they called for their glasses to be filled.

Half an hour later, a woman with a shaven head, wearing only a thong and a flowing robe, twirled through the room, introducing her breasts to each of the guests.

Simone raised her eyebrows and clutched her champagne flute. She had expected a nice little tea dance with the old ladies waltzing under a glitter ball. She hadn't expected a nude exhibitionist. Simone had known that her grandmother was a lesbian since Simone was very young, and the few gala events she had witnessed convinced her that the woman certainly lead the high life. But it hadn't occurred to her that this type of licentiousness had been taking place. She wasn't sure she wanted to know this about her grandmother. But events were transpiring without her having a vote in them, that was for certain. She had to know how her grandmother had lived and was reveling in the feeling of being her grandmother, but it put her in a position where she couldn't pick and choose the information. It was a price she would have to pay, squeamish or not.

The old women motioned Simone to the sofa where she joined Jana. The doorbell rang again. Music began. Dancers twirled around the room wearing masks of brightly colored leather adorned with feathers and beads, torn slips and mismatched stockings, tattoos of Celtic crosses, and little else. The maid lit a roaring fire, then stripped down to her panties and bra and strode around the room holding a champagne bottle by its neck and running her fingers over the bare backs of the dancers. Simone could have gotten up and gone to the room they had prepared for her. She could have called a cab and left altogether, but she was drunk and curious. Besides, she wanted to see Abigail, to be the bit of Abigail everyone said she was, and so she joined Jana in laughing and saluting the dancers, admiring their thighs, their breasts, comparing preferences. Other guests arrived who kissed the older women, then filled plates, poured drinks, and danced. They ripped off their shirts and let their breasts bounce in the candlelight.

Jana called for additional dancers and drummers until the room held more than three dozen people—guests, dancers, and Jana's staff indistinguishable from one another, the drums setting a rhythm for the room. The dancers rode each other's hips in time to the music, ran bright threads through each other's nipple rings, and tied themselves together like a string ball. They laid themselves head to toe on the floor and sucked each other off. Jana flung a leg over the sofa arm and begged her maid to fuck herself while sitting on Jana's lap. The dancers tumbled over furniture, lifting their legs to expose their labia, dancing with their ankles high in the air, plunging fingers inside themselves.

Simone slipped into a haze as the smell of champagne and candles wafted through the rooms. A naked woman draped herself across the coffee table in front of the sofa and the dancers closed in. With their hands clutching each other's breasts, rhythmically pulling their pubic hair, four dancers flanked the supine woman with white paraffin candles and dribbled her with rivers of wax. Simone felt the heat and slipped her hand inside her blouse. The flanking dancers pulled the woman to her feet and tied her hands to the mantel pillars nearby. The fire blazed. With the wax still clinging to her, the woman undulated to the music, her loose ties allowing her to slide up and down the pillars, spread her legs and crouch, raise herself up and shove her ass far out behind her. The drumming increased in pitch and speed.

There were now so many people in the room that it appeared to be a frenzy of arms, legs, and nipples, as if the room itself were whirling around her. The old women were bright eyes and laughing mouths, lost under fabric and nubile bodies. Women folded themselves over tables and chairs, undulating in rhythm with the woman tied to the pillars. Simone felt as if the room and the evening had taken on a life of its own, uncontrollable, building in intensity as dancers lined up behind the beckoning ass of another dancer, stroking legs and backs, pressing pelvis into buttocks. The lights dimmed as the last G-string was stripped off. Simone panted, unable to move. This was not like sex she had ever had. She was caught in the pull of sex, without control, vulnerable to someone else's direction. She was lost in the white water of it.

All the drummers turned in the direction of the door at the far side the room. Hooded and robed in radiant blue satin, a dancer entered and moved through the room draping the blue cape over each couple, hiding them, thrusting with them, then twirling away to leave them diving hands, fingers, dildos into pussies.

The woman tied to the pillars, unable to see the other figures, moved with their moans and the wet open sound of their thrusting. The blue figure stood at the fireplace, the leaping flames lighting up the cape. The other couples in the room made a din of moans and near climaxes. The hooded figure twirled in a circle until the blue cape opened to expose white skin and blurred, indistinct flesh. The woman tied to the mantel pulled at her restraints in her desire to watch.

With one motion, the blue-clad dancer leapt forward. As the bound woman leaned backward to strain against the ties, the blue dancer thrust into her, pelvis smacking into the bound woman's fleshy buttocks, driving deep. The two lovers took the moans of the room with them, the night of vision, the old women's memories, the fire into the flesh—boring into Simone's indecision and formlessness.

Simone, the drums and alcohol in possession of her mind, pulled the maid off Jana's lap and the two rolled to the floor. Simone thrust into the maid in time with the blue dancer, in rhythm with the room, leaving her own innocence and seizing her future, biting into her identity and hunger.

In the morning, Simone woke with a start and unfolded herself from the sofa. An old woman was sleeping in a lounge chair and a few of the dancers were still curled on the tables and chairs where they had come. The bound woman and the blue-clad dancer, still in the hood, were entangled in each other's arms at the base of the fireplace. Simone struggled to her feet and tucked in her shirt.

The maid, clad only in a small see-through apron, intercepted her with a cup of coffee. Simone took her chin and kissed her deeply, as if experimenting, wondering who she would be and what country she would be in when she opened her eyes. The maid pushed her gently backward and kissed her lightly on the cheek.

Simone gathered her rucksack upstairs, folded her grandmother's shirt into one of the pockets, and came down the stairs to find Jana with her friends, the three of them in long robes, each clutching a mug of tea.

"Are you leaving us so soon?" Jana said.

"I need to get back to Nana."

"Of course. But dance with us again soon? Many times, my little chip of Abigail, many times."

At the train station, Simone found a phone.

"Nana...I have a report on the...dance," Simone said, furtively looking around the train station.

"Ah, there was dancing," the old woman said dreamily. "Did you dance, my dearest?"

Simone was quiet and embarrassed. "I did, Nana."

"Quite a gift, is it not?"

Simone shifted uneasily, tried to corral her unruly mop. "Are you well? How are you feeling?"

"Happy to get your message," her grandmother said weakly. "Would you go to Prague for me to see another friend?"

*S*imone took a boat from Stockholm to Prague. Visions of the bacchanal followed her, bursting out of the swells of ocean water. Again and again Simone saw the woman tied to the mantelpiece offering up her cunt, her soft butt in the air, the dancer in the blue cape lunging into her. Simone felt fucked by every wave that slapped against the side of the boat. She saw her reflection in the boat's windows, her wild hair whipped in the wind like the flames around the bound woman. She had never been involved in sex like that before.

During college, sex was something she had after a few dates, a prize she was given after she displayed an appropriate level of sincerity and commitment. It was booty stolen behind the guise of drink. *A gift,* her grandmother had said, and Simone laughed and laid her cheek against the cold boat railing. *Freely given, not earned.* The maid was the first woman Simone had fucked without knowing, really. She supposed she should feel guilty, buy her a gift, send her a card or call her when she reached port. But that would certainly spoil it, wouldn't it? The maid had pushed her away when Simone had tried to hold her as if they had some connection. If Simone could live with the guilt, she could preserve the maid as her first mystery and so make the sex pristine, uncluttered by facts and personalities, relationships. The dance would be her first gift.

She bought a postcard on the boat and penned a note to her grandmother: *Not a prize hard-fought and captured, or earned through arduous similarity, passion is a gift freely given, carnival beads flung into the crowd.*

In Prague, she announced herself to an older woman whose eyes glazed over with memories at the mention of Abigail's name. Simone had dinner with the woman and her friends, listened to their stories, held them while they cried over the pending loss of her grandmother. When Simone called her grandmother, the old woman asked her for descriptions of the river, of the light above the central church, sent her out again on adventures so she could describe the smell of pastries on a certain street.

"General delivery," her grandmother weakly instructed her. Another name, another destination at general delivery.

Simone pursued her task, envelope to envelope. Seven countries yielded seven lovers. She made love with a friend of the woman whose name was in the envelope, then a snooty niece, the secretary of the message recipient, a caterer. She had varied the pattern just to find out what exactly made the envelopes arrive: the sex, the delivery of the message, or the descriptions she gave her grandmother afterward. The envelopes and the money continued. At each stop, Simone pieced together another part of her grandmother's life and so, she felt, her own past. She began to approach destinations and people as if she had been there. She called her grandmother with details, and dropped postcards in the mail. Phyllis said they were the best medicine her grandmother had.

Today as she stretched her long legs in the train, she laughed out loud. She had a degree in Medieval Culture, and that would allow her to work as a clerk or a waitress, if she were lucky. She hadn't bothered to make plans for herself. People had been making them for her entire life and it had left her without the ability to choose her own direction. Now her grandmother had given her freedom, a life in which she made love to women around the world with no concern for money. She was deliriously free.

Simone felt that the train speeding along was her, cutting through the drudgery that others had to endure, flying through a life of endless possibilities and wide-open time. People labored in the fields around her. They brought her extravagant lunches and afternoon brandies. She ate and drank in the first-class cabins, in the first-class restaurants with the working rich, men whose lives were trapped in briefcases and calculators, the hollowness of their eyes revealing that they, too, operated in repetitive cycles.

She leaned her head against the starched linen headrest of the train seat and closed her eyes. The movement of the train became her back rocking under mosquito netting. Her arm dropping off the seat was the languishing gesture of the moment she gave in to being laid across a table. The train coursing around a corner was the time a lover had spun her through Mediterranean water until the sea and the sky had only her naked body between them for definition.

Simone's life had no walls. She spent her time at the opera, museums, promenades, art studios, theaters. In the markets sipping coffee, on the rural hillside looking for the shepherdess, in the stacks introducing herself to the librarian, in the lab seducing the chemist. She lounged on sofas and beds inventing new ways to approach, caress, lunge, bite, take a woman to the place where she unhinged herself, as Simone liked to think of it, separating her thinking mind from her body, divorcing the logical brain from the dark and amorphous place where the woman became the surrendering animal.

When she found the women on her grandmother's list, their families and friends looked on Simone as though she were a Bodhisattva, a visitor returning to lift them from the banality of their daily lives. To bestow on them a spark of sacredness, as if chosen for a special ritual. It was what they knew of her grandmother, explained as the Fitzwater legacy, and she was more than willing to carry it on. Women turned from their husbands, suddenly felt beautiful, empowered, emboldened, and adorned. Simone was lavish with her money, leaving them with new cars, college educations for their daughters, or pieces of property to hedge against their old age. More money was just an envelope away.

In a way, Simone felt that she owed it to them. She was more alive than ever. She became aroused each time she knocked on another door. She moved through the houses, her six-foot stride gobbling up the floor, with an eye to each woman in the room: who will be my lover now? Her posture was impeccable. Her movements were languorous, infused with the tension of someone who is waiting, poised and confident. She was electric. Simone's nipples were erect all day and night. She walked down unknown streets with the nerve endings in her vulva tingling, her movements driven by the gnawing center of her body. She drank coffee with slightly pursed lips that were full and moist, as if she were seconds away from a kiss. Her hands fidgeted around a wine glass, thirsty for a wrist, a thigh, a breast. Simone had become predatory in her fixation on sex, and it was the most alive she had ever felt. They had rescued her, these women on this list, and the other women she discovered during the pursuit, given her a direction. A purpose. Now she lived for her labia, her clitoris, for the sweat and the moans and the gratitude of the late night.

*I*n London, Simone raised her hand to the bell as if she had a vaporous trail of sexual energy flowing like a cape from her broad shoulders. She delivered her message over biscuits and bone china to an aging woman who spun tales of Abigail, catacombs, a carriage house, a clandestine party, white gloves, top hats. Back on the misty street, Simone felt a hunger in her chest. She needed a hand across her cheek, the fine hair of belly-down across her lips, a sweaty and insistent thigh tight around her back. She wandered the streets, the flat grey night a sharp contrast to her scorching need.

She entered a bistro, stripped off her coat with resignation, then turned at the sound of a woman's impassioned voice and the catcalls of her detractors.

"How can you challenge me?" the woman shouted to her companions who were crowded around a table spilling over with beer mugs and empty plates. She paced behind them, raising her arms in protest. "Humans are the only animals on the planet willing to live without passion."

A reveler at the head of the table threw back his head and waved her away. Two others let their words drown each other out in happy derision. They were a threadbare lot, unkempt and drunk. The orator paced behind them, a woman with close-cropped hair and green eyes that could pierce metal. She wore a physician's lab coat covered with paint splatters, the T-shirt underneath it torn at the collar. As Simone neared the table, she thought the speaker smelled of turpentine and cinnamon. It made her want the woman.

"A water buffalo, Anna," a drunken companion challenged. "What's the passion of a water buffalo?"

"Or a goat?" slurred another. "Are they driven by desire?"

"Perhaps what she means," Simone interrupted, "is that we're the only animals with more brains than passion to direct us."

"Ah-ha," the orator said, slamming down her beer mug and struggling to Simone's side. "Our intruder has hit it square on now." She took Simone's arm as if they were going to promenade. "The only animals whose stupidity doesn't perfectly match their desire. Just enough brains to want grass but nothing more."

A din of protest rose from the table. Anna clutched Simone's arm tighter. "Do you see passion driving this world?" She waved dramatically to the window where fog obliterated the view. "Is England spilling over with people who go forth with passion in their hearts?"

Someone handed Simone a mug of beer and wrapped an arm around her neck to persuade her of the opposing view.

"And create from a place of desire? Drudgery—that's the state religion," Anna shouted, bending over the table for even greater dramatic effect but nearly falling into the beer. Simone wanted to see the passion this woman could bring to her bed. She joined the group, bought a round, kept close to the orator's side.

The next morning, armed with the address of Anna's painting studio and her schedule, Simone bought a bottle of good champagne and some orange juice and set out.

Anna was surprised to see Simone and let her in tentatively.

"I'm afraid we were all a bit crocked last night," Anna said sheepishly, then returned to her canvas as if Simone might be delivering Chinese food and leaving.

Simone stepped into the studio in a long leather coat and riding boots, reiterating their agreement to meet, but Anna sketched shapes on a canvas with a pencil, her back to Simone, making only grunting sounds to acknowledge that noise had been created in her space.

"I was very taken by your comments about desire," Simone said, stepping closer to Anna.

Anna nodded absently, bent over her work.

"And especially by the fervor with which you believe them."

Anna looked up and quickly leaned away, startled by how close Simone was. "Could you…," she said, holding up her smudged hand and waving Simone away, "move to the…."

Simone turned but saw nothing behind her. The walls were blank except for the splattered outline of previous paintings, and the paint-encrusted table in front of her was empty. She wondered what was she blocking, but stepped aside nonetheless.

"The light…" Anna said distractedly. "Unusual in London."

Simone was at a loss.

"Actually, I didn't say *desire*," Anna pointed out, holding up a single finger and looking Simone in the eyes for the first time. "There's plenty of desire in the world."

"Is there in yours?" Simone asked, setting down the champagne and orange juice, then leaning on the table to let Anna see she had no shirt on underneath her long coat.

Anna paused. "Are you trying to seduce me?"

Simone crossed her legs, put her hands behind her so that her leather coat gaped wider. "Trying."

"How very flattering. Thank you," Anna said, wiping her hands on a paint rag from her pocket.

Simone opened the champagne and when she offered the orange juice, Anna waved it away, took the glass straight.

"But I *didn't* say desire," Anna admonished. "The world is rife with desire, the longing, the hunger of desire. I said passion, which is entirely different." She took a big swallow, set the glass down, and moved to shelves where she rummaged for paints. "Passion isn't formless longing. It is a drive to know why you are here and once you know that, to fulfill the mission."

"Desire is all take," she continued, going back to her easel. "Passion is more a state of giving. Desire can be incessant and unchanging—a meal following another meal following another meal." Anna tossed aside the pencil and, nearly ignoring Simone's presence, brought stacks of paint cans to the table. "But passion insists that you grow, change, improve. Passion drives progress—the need for better, not just more. A passion for justice for a people. A passion to be a better painter. A better parent. Passion is work, desire is indulgence.

"It takes courage to have a passion—enormous courage." Anna slammed down a can of paint and seized a screwdriver as if it were a lethal weapon. "And the incessant application of that courage. Desire, on the other hand, is simple repetition."

Anna stopped abruptly, set down her brushes, and walked toward Simone, who was leaning against the table, her skin and intentions visible.

"This certainly took courage," Anna whispered, running her fingers down Simone's lapel, then slowly pulling open the coat to expose her breasts. Simone was burning. Anna untied the belt and regarded Simone's belly, her muff and thighs. When Simone didn't pull away, Anna exhaled deeply. She looked around the studio, brought a cushion and pillows to a lone empty table in the center of the room, and motioned Simone to lay herself out as her model. Anna propped up the canvas bearing her pencil sketches, repositioned herself behind her easel, and looked in Simone's direction. Then she began painting.

Simone was naked except for her tall black riding boots. Anna came to her, spread Simone's legs, and positioned her against the pillows so that she was laid across a streak of sunshine. Fueled by Anna's words and her own nudity, Simone spread her legs and let her blood sing over her display. She could be delivered from her girlhood of longing, pining away for her mother and grandmother; she could be naked and newborn into a life where her passion was passion itself.

Simone stretched into the pillows, ran her hand from her lapel, across her breast, her belly, into her muff.

"That's nice," Anna said. "Yes, leave your hand right there."

To be here with Anna, feeling the glorious, wrenching effort of the woman's art. The air reeked of turpentine and pigment. She could feel Anna's stillness, then the emergence of an idea, the tentative sketch of it against the canvas followed by the frenzied application of paint. Anna's excitement built until she stopped mid-stroke, stood back, questioning, then rested and began a new exploration. Anna and her passion. Simone sensed the woman's gaze sweeping across her skin, the woman's brush explaining her body. She teased her fingers across her labia while Anna chose another brush, watched her, turned back to the painting. Simone felt that she was truly seen, that her quest and her lust were pouring from her and being translated into color. She threw her head back, pulled her labia forward, arched her back and moaned. She heard the soft scrape of brush against canvas, slipped her fingers inside and rocked herself forward.

"Your hair is the most amazing color," Anna said, walking behind Simone. Anna's proximity and Simone's blatant display brought a flush to Simone's neck. She closed her eyes and lay motionless, her fingers inside her. "Licorice. A true black." Anna buried her face in the wild mane of hair. "God, that I could smell this color," she said, gripping the curls until Simone could feel the pinch on her clitoris.

The two women parried, Simone hanging on the edge of a climax, Anna struggling forward with her vision. Simone watched Anna strain, heard the viscous paint oozing onto the woman's palette. Then, with a little yelp, Anna looked up at the windows and noticed that the light had begun to change. She became frenzied to finish the painting, and Simone worked her clitoris until she climaxed. Anna, satisfied, stood back from the painting and lit a cigarette.

Opening her eyes and drinking in the stillness of the room,

Simone sipped champagne from the bottle, got off the table, and retied her coat. She handed the bottle to Anna, who took an enormous swig that left her breathless. Anna wiped her mouth on the edge of her sleeve and smiled at Simone. She reached up and pulled Simone's face to her lips, kissed her, then turned back to her painting. Simone followed her.

"Is that…me?" Simone was incredulous over the abstraction in front of her.

"No." Anna chuckled, "I only paint abstractions. But it was nice to look up at someone who was following their passion." She carried the canvas to the spot just behind the table where Simone had lain. "Is that it?" she asked herself. "Nearly. Yes, there's the light," she said, holding the painting into the streak of sunshine. "There it is! No. But nearly." She set the canvas aside, picked up another one and put it on her easel. "Maybe less yellow this time."

That night, drunken and morose over her foolish exhibition and self-aggrandizement, Simone sent a postcard to her grandmother: *Tough lessons tell me that passion gives the world its drive; desire gives the world its pain. Where is my passion, Nana? Bring me home.*

S imone tossed uncomfortably on the couch in her grandmother's room as the old woman's coughing racked
Simone's own chest. Sunshine poured through the windows, and competing orchestral music—day and
night at her grandmother's order—could be heard from
every room of the house. Stravinsky strings fighting with Bach
harpsichord. Phyllis would barely speak to Simone and when
she did, her disappointment over Simone's abandonment of
the task tainted her words. Besides, Simone was disappointed
herself. Her return had stripped her of her purpose and
Anna's words kept ringing in her head reminding her that passion was not passive.

Simone ordered the staff to remove everything from her
room that hadn't come from her own life. All the paintings and
objects were taken away. She unpacked her books from college, hung her few blouses, chinos, and jeans, and laid the ticket
stubs from the Stockholm Baths, several theater bills and
carved boxes onto her dresser. Her barren monk's cell made
it clear that as yet she had no life of her own and its accusa-
tion drove her to her grandmother's room. But it was just as
impossible to sit idly by while her nana became listless and with-
drawn, sinking deeper and deeper toward death. The pain of
losing the last woman in her life, robbing her nana of the elixir

that was extending her life, sent Simone pacing through the house in tears. And to lose her grandmother without yet knowing who she was, perhaps leaving Simone in this big house with all her possessions but none of her memories, finally convinced Simone to pack her rucksack and present herself to Phyllis.

"All right, I'll go," Simone said, "but you have to promise me one thing: you'll tell me the time frame associated with these women, the years Nana spent with them. I have to have a thread here, Phyllis."

"Agreed," Phyllis said, relieved.

"And so I am exploring…"

"Your grandmother's forty-fifth year."

"And that stop would be…"

"Belgium," Phyllis said, withdrawing an envelope from her pocket and placing it in Simone's hand, which she gripped tightly in gratitude.

Simone flew to Belgium with a small brown leather notebook in her lap, inscribing the names and locations of her previous destinations, the women's names, the activities. She tried to create two columns, one with her grandmother's friends and one with her own, but soon found that they overlapped and her memory was strained enough to write down the names of all the women she had made love to, let alone remember how she had met them. Delivering her message in Belgium, she poured over photograph books of her grandmother, asked questions in simple English, and attempted to piece together the answers. She relayed information to Phyllis, then called the next day to learn that her grandmother was greatly heartened by the news of her old friend.

Because Simone had a number of names to contact in New York, she took up temporary residence at a small bed and breakfast in Chelsea. She was glad to immerse herself in her own culture and still feed her grandmother's reminiscences, spending her days wandering the streets of the Village, her nights at soirees overlooking Central Park. New York was filthy and it stank, with garbage choking the gutters and the sidewalks, but it was America. The billboards and newspapers called to her in her own language, and she began to feel like an ordinary woman with a newspaper, a yogurt, and a subway token. She strolled Greene Street from the bookstore to the cafe and back again.

She was reading a book after dinner when the waitress set a snifter of brandy next to her coffee cup. Simone looked up the long expanse of the woman's arm, up the downy skin to the lace of her bra, then to her face, and before she knew what she was doing, Simone reached out and grabbed the woman's hand.

The waitress, startled, stood wide-eyed and stuffed her other hand into her apron pocket. Simone pretended to shake her hand as a way to explain her abruptness but, in fact, she could hardly imagine letting go. Simone wanted to sink her teeth into the woman's flesh and gobble her down like a kid with a chocolate Easter rabbit, feel the woman break under her teeth and melt on her tongue. She gripped the woman's forearm hungrily. Then, apologetically, Simone let go and watched her work the last of the evening's patrons, people who had agreed to desserts they didn't touch, who pressed large tips into her palm as they left. Old women kissed her cheeks and old men her hands. It wasn't that any one part of her was breathtaking—eyes, skin, legs—though she was luscious, with long curly red hair and full lips, breasts that invited hands. It was that for some reason she possessed the ability to warm you, Simone decided. She made you long to have her wrap you up in her coat and keep you. Simone, suddenly enormously weary, wanted to throw her arms around the woman's waist and bury herself in her skirt.

She set down her coffee cup, checked to see how tangled her mop of hair really was, ran her tongue across her teeth, and marshaled all her forces toward the woman. If ever she had given herself to a woman, if ever she had thought she was capable of seduction, this was the moment to prove it, the time when all skills and finesse she had acquired from the road were needed. Simone, unable to identify a specific body part that she craved, longed to tear open her own shirt and offer the woman her warm skin. Her tongue ached to be taken.

"Do you need more coffee?" the waitress said.

"Would you join me?" Simone said.

"I don't usually…but it is closing time." She waved at the last patron who looked as if he were being torn from his childhood sweetheart.

"Naomi," she said, offering her hand again.

"Simone," she said, shaking it anew, feeling herself melt into the woman's grip. If she could just draw her to the floor and cup her head, pull the woman on top of her....What was going to be her strategy? she wondered, shifting in her seat with excitement.

"You look tired, Simone."

"I've been traveling a lot," Simone said in a sultry tone, trotting out her standard mysterious line and expecting to spin an alluring tale of world-class cities and their magic.

"And who is sending you on this journey?" Naomi said.

Simone stopped with the coffee cup in mid-air. "How did you know someone was sending me?" She had lost all her sultriness.

"Vacationers sleep," Naomi said.

Simone fell into the dark tunnels of Naomi's eyes, tumbling into her gaze.

"My grandmother…," Simone began, realizing that she had never mentioned her situation to anyone who hadn't already known of it. "My grandmother is dying and she's asked me to visit her friends and tell them of her love for them."

"How gracious. Where did your grandmother live?"

"Everywhere. Absolutely everywhere," Simone exclaimed. "I've been to fourteen countries already and have only covered a few years of her life."

Naomi raised her eyebrows, then nodded her head. "That's very devoted of you. Are you all right?"

"She's all I have," Simone said, her eyes suddenly filling with tears. "I don't have myself. I only have…her."

"Maybe we should get some air," Naomi said with concern, and stood.

Despite Simone's towering height, she took Naomi's arm and allowed herself to be supported as they walked down the street, the words spilling from her mouth, Simone stumbling as if tripping on them. She told Naomi about her mother and her fear of the outside world, the quiet intimacy of the two of them spooning on the couch; she cried about her mother's death until Naomi had to sit her on a park bench until she collected herself. The woman's curly red hair brushed against Simone's face as she put her arm around her shoulder, and Simone wanted to hide in the forest of it, wanted to live in the fragile sweetness of the woman's neck. The words came out in a jumble as they walked the streets, then climbed the stairs to Naomi's apartment. Simone talked about the postcards and the nights in boarding school, the shock of the bacchanal in Stockholm, her need for a home, the old ladies with their tea cups and doilies, the fantastic sex, the wanderlust, the sound of her stepfather's ice. When she finally stopped sobbing and explaining and backtracking to make sense of her story, she felt as if Naomi had taken a saber and split her from pubis to sternum.

"Come in for a bit," Naomi whispered, standing above Simone on one of the steps. She took Simone's chin and kissed her tear-salty lips, pulled her to her chest, and let her curly hair fall over Simone's face. "I have a chaise lounge on the roof. View of all Manhattan. Let me hold you," she whispered into Simone's ear, sending her breath all the way down to Simone's clit.

Simone backed away, pulled Naomi's arms from around

her neck. Sex would be sacrilegious, she thought. It was a sport, and this was not a woman to enlist in the game. But even as she explained this to herself, Simone knew the truth: exposing something other than her body was clumsy fumbling in Simone's hands. This liaison didn't have the anonymity of the envelopes. She had exposed more of herself and her labyrinths than she had with anyone in the world, and it simply made sex too dangerous. She backed down the stairs.

"You're leaving?" Naomi was incredulous. Simone pressed Naomi's hands between hers, bowed gallantly, and started down the sidewalk.

"Hey, I don't just invite anybody up, you know!" Naomi called after her, then abashedly looked up and down the street. "New York!" she growled, throwing open the door to her apartment building. "Full of psychopaths."

imone flew to Sydney and made love to several women using the fervor she had felt for Naomi, seeing Naomi's hair when she closed her eyes, imagining her comfort as she rolled over to sleep in another woman's arms.

She wrote a postcard to her grandmother: *The past forward to the future. Each lover lost is there in the touch given the next, no woman the first, as we, even as virgins, had mothers.*

Calling Boston, she reported to her grandmother that the friend she had searched for had died, that the bird sanctuary her nana had established was still thriving, but that the lace shop she had inquired about had been replaced by a T-shirt joint. She apologized to Phyllis for the ill effect that the news might have on her grandmother, and told her to send the next envelope to San Francisco, where she was going to wait for her orders.

San Francisco was raining, wintry, yet the buds were bursting on the trees and the new grass was fluorescent green. Each day she watched the thick white fog cover the hills as if it were her own hand pulling a sheet over her breasts, alone in her bed, time and again reenacting her inability to mingle vulnerability and sex, sex and intimacy.

She wandered through Hayes Valley, downhearted, sipping

on a cup of coffee and window-shopping. The fog had moved in so thick and fast that the ends of the streets disappeared and the world became limited to just what was in front of her in the store windows. After passing by an art glass dealership and a leather goods shop, Simone stopped in front of an antiques place that had a window at the top of a short stoop. She watched a carousel with a wooden lion, ostrich, and cat with a fish in its mouth circle in front of her and felt her spirits spiraling downward. Around and around she went—a breast, a cunt, a hip, a hand—love as wooden as these animals on poles.

A woman with hair tucked under a cloche, wearing a belted suit from the forties, leaned into the window display to adjust a collection of brooches. Simone thought she moved like a ghost, barely skimming the surface of the tin motorcycles and colored bottles on display. She was so perfectly appointed in the dress and make-up of the forties, with the fog so thick around the window, that Simone felt as if she was looking into a rip in time. She was peering into another era, decades ago, and half expected her grandmother to be standing at the back desk counting bills onto the tabletop. Simone wanted to walk into that other place and find sanctuary, slip her hand into her grandmother's.

The woman in the window leaned over far enough for Simone to see the fluted ruffles of her bra in the V-neck of her suit. The woman reached down, opened a miniature wooden box with a tiny mirror on the inside of its lid, and held it in the palm of her hand at just the level of her cleavage that enabled Simone to see her own eye. Simone's eye framed by the woman's breasts made her tongue involuntarily twitch within her mouth. The woman set the box down again, then picked up another and opened the lid. A green enameled lizard rose and started to turn. The woman set it down to twirl in the corner of the window and found yet another box, this one containing a tiger, which she set to spin in the opposite corner. Then there was a third that held a bear. The woman noticed Simone and raised her heavily painted eyes to her, proffering a small, carved box which she placed in the palm of her hand as she had the box with the mirror. Hesitating to be sure she had Simone's attention, she slowly opened the lid. The figure of a naked woman rose from the box, carved from blonde wood with one hand flung over her head and the other deep in her cunt. Turning to music Simone couldn't hear, the figure undulated in an uneven orbit, turning within the confines of the shopkeeper's cleavage. Simone tossed her coffee into a trash bin and took the stairs two at a time.

She wanted no details, vowed to refuse all questions on her past, her childhood, her zodiac sign or taste in music. She longed for an envelope to send her on her way but would settle for this stranger with the little cloche and the window into the past until the woman began to ask questions.

The shopkeeper continued to hold the naked woman between her breasts as Simone slipped her hand over the waistband of her tailored suit and down her tight, smooth buttocks. She smelled faintly of brandy in the middle of the afternoon. As they kissed, Simone heard the little animals, one by one, run out of music and spring, descending into their tiny boxes, the lids snapping shut. Simone held the back of the woman's head without mussing her hair or disturbing her hat and kissed her as if the woman could transport her through the fog and the peek-a-boo windows to the time when her grandmother would still decide to come home and love a little orphan girl.

The shopkeeper pushed the naked figure back into her box, set it carelessly on the windowsill, and led Simone by the hand into the rear of the shop, past tufted chairs and sideboards with claw feet. She pulled a heavy curtain across the door behind them and laid herself out on the single cot.

Her name was Meg, the woman said without elaboration, and tore the buttons off Simone's shirt. Simone didn't care about a lock on the front of the shop or a door to the room; they were in a different world and perhaps she had become a ghost as well. The wind howled outside, chilling the old Victorian building. They dove under a down comforter and fucked until they wound up on the floor tangled in sheets and silk stockings, got up and showered in the store bathroom to heat their bones, then scurried into bed again until their lips were puffy from kissing and their skin raw with riding each other's legs. Their hairlines were sweaty, their mouths dry. They needed food, they needed water, and they tore apart Meg's shop kitchen, screwing on the butcher block, shoving all the remnants of their dinner onto the floor.

In the morning, Simone looked fearfully at Meg as she slept. Maybe this ghost woman from the past wouldn't ask her to stay and share the bathrobe side of life, the yogurt and bill-paying side. Just to be sure, though, she picked up her jacket, and scribbled a note: *Write me general delivery in London.* Simone left without a sound.

She wrote Meg a letter about her breasts and sent it from

the airport. When she got to London she wrote her a description of her smooth, round buttocks as they looked when Simone was fucking her. Simone wrote her letters while sitting in cafes, biding her time, capturing her lust on paper. She had no purpose in London, no envelope, no reason to be there except to avoid falling into the trap she had barely avoided with Naomi. Absence was what made sex grow hotter, and absence was what she would provide.

A month later, she showed up at Meg's store ten minutes before closing, unannounced except for the jingle of the front door shutting behind her. When Meg tried to ask her where she had been, Simone laid her out for hours on the rug of the shop only a few feet from the front door. The next morning, without a word, Simone got on a plane back to London.

Simone arrived and disappeared another half a dozen times, and at each visit Meg seemed so completely immured in the past that Simone expected to find her in bed cutting out World War II ration coupons, talking about the youngster Babe Ruth. There was a comfort in it for Simone, as if her quest for the past and her confinement in the present had melded for once. She was able to sleep deeply, united and at rest. When she crawled into Meg's arms, she gathered the past around her like a blanket.

Then one night Meg brought in a plate of cookies on some ancient china and, brushing away Simone's hand as it slid into her robe, asked Simone to describe her hometown and tell her what she did for a living. Simone didn't answer, kissed Meg's mouth until her lips bled, cinched her trousers, and left for London.

After sending Meg another score of letters filled with descriptions of their sex, Simone got a reply.

> *My dearest Simone,*
>
> *Someday you will get off the plane and I will take your hand as it hangs by your side, raise it to my lips to kiss the palm that has always only waved good-bye, kiss the hand that has often held a pen but rarely held me. You will be here, with me. Mine, finally is what my heart will say over and over. Mine, finally. My lips into your palm, your strong fingers across my cheeks and nose. Do you know now that the mention of a plane brings me visions of your wrist and the way I will hold it at the base of my throat, sleep with the tips of your fingers curled in trust under my chin, your arm in the space between my grateful breasts?*
>
> *Hurry to see me. Make plans. Tell me you'll be here. These letters are beginning to show a woman forging hope into desperation. We are the stuff of sex and passion, my darling, that is who we are, and must be. Send me faint gesture of a train ticket, a glimmer of a plane reservation. I await your arrival. Be finally, adventuring.*

Simone paced aimlessly through London with Meg's letter in her pocket, its courtly formality keeping her linked with the past, comforting her. She arrived the following week and dragged Meg straight into the kitchen. One tiny piece of information per visit, that was all that Simone would allow. There would be no mistakes this time. I'm from Boston, Simone said curtly, and I will show you my purpose in life.

She made Meg pull her favorite foods from the cupboard and line them up on the butcher block. Simone pulled off her shirt, stripped off her bra, and picked up a butter knife from the chopping block. She twisted the lid off the honey-mustard jar and smeared a dollop in the hollow of her collar bone. Meg leapt on her, sucking the mustard from her skin. Simone knifed hazelnut Nuttella into her cleavage and Meg pulled her own dress off, wrapping her legs around Simone's waist as she licked the sweet paste from her chest. Meg sucked raisin chutney from Simone's navel, brandied bananas from her shoulder blades, honey from her labia. They dripped chocolate into each other's mouths, until Simone rolled them over and fucked her with the vegetables.

In the morning, Meg was left with a filthy kitchen and labia that throbbed. She wrote general delivery, London.

> *My dearest Simone,*
> *Today as I walked through my shop, my dress cried out to you. It is a new frock, unseasonably light and flowing for this fog-bound city. It played with my thighs, slipped across my buttocks. My dress moved across the rounds of my breasts and my nipples called your name, singing. Today, as I surveyed my customers, I dreamt of the nape of your neck, of the down that leads me into the silk of your hair, of my lips accepting the invitation, my tongue behind your ear. Across five*

thousand kilometers, the shadow of your body presses into mine and tells me (dare I say it?) that we need to be together. Not just in thoughts, in the fleeting moments when the memory of you and the languid sex we shared makes me forget that I am tallying books. Not just in midnights that are so sweet and tangled that I awake, certain you are bringing strawberries from the next room. Not just in the sudden feel of your hands moving up my thighs, trembling with the need to pretend that they do not know where they're going and aren't in a hurry to get there.

Be my lover, Simone. Let me see you in the morning wrestling with dreams of bag ladies or trees that cry. Let me catch you absently staring out the window, the light warming your skin. You are scowling and don't notice your beauty, not then, not when you're ironing in your bra, or driving. Surely there is a way to capture this passion we have, the desire that makes the paper in these envelopes crackle. Your letters are my bones, they hold me together, they are the strength I need. Your letters arrive and, mere paper, they manage to be your hands, gruffly clasping my face to draw me to your lips, forceful with their passion. My dream, my precious, how can you dominate me with paper? How can you make me yield, collapsing under the sweet drug of my submission, wanting nothing more than to lie down and receive your skill? I sleep with your letter clutched in my hand, as if it could approximate the warmth of flesh.

But my dearest, my love, you have to know, something is different now. I used to litter my bed with your letters until it was more paper than sheet, and rise in the morning singing over the wealth of our love, of the attention, the climax each postmark signified. Showering, I was careful of the water, as if each inch of my life was covered with precious envelopes and words that should never be blurred. The memory of our fiery times together has kept me alive. Your neck has turned to receive my lips a thousand times since its muscles actually moved.

Now I ask you, what is the price of this passion? I look at our letters and they seem so thin, not infused with the blood and heat of flesh. I am sad. There. I've said it. I ache with the pain of something I can't identify. If I ask you to meet me, to make more memories— our usual way of dulling this pain—it simply prolongs what we know is true. And the ache is different this time. I don't just want you. I want us. Oh, I can hear what you say: that the tension of our separation fuels our passion. That those who know the realities of laundry soap and nasal sprays do not know the ecstasy of the flawless hunger that we have. I can see you pacing in my little bedroom, my pubic hairs clinging to unlikely spots on you. You pontificate: "Consensus is the death of seduction." Your reasoning, and the furious sex you give me later, have kept me.

Is the price of our passion this paper-thin love? Is the distance really what makes the sex burn so bright?

You must ask yourself, my darling, which is the fuel—the paper, or the love? If it is the love, it would survive. But if it is the paper, is the isolation a price worth paying?

Write to me, my darling, and as I always close with a plea to see you, I ask you to take me in your arms, my love. Be finally, here.

Simone became frantic. It wasn't just the distance or the sex; time itself had become a fuel for the passion. How could she explain to Meg that her membership in a different era was as enticing as her pert breasts and firm nipples? Simone wrote her another dozen letters about food, about sex, about the way her body looked when the seacoast sky came in her bedroom window. She made no mention of an arrival date. She didn't book a flight. It would be the half-hearted gesture of a sheet pulled over a nipple, the covering of their passion if she saw Meg now. A single correspondence from Meg arrived later that month.

My dearest,

You are coming, aren't you? My heart is pacing back and forth in my chest. You are arriving, yes? I am standing in such infuriating passivity, as if at an elevator that will not arrive, a plane circling endlessly, toast that will not golden-brown. I stomp my foot time and again in the shop and the customers put their heads down, looking like I've caught them touching crystal too delicate for their thick and bullish fingers. What can I tell

them: I'm anxious for my lover? For the arrival of the
one who makes the sweat slick my body, who cuts my
breath into short bursts with a simple move of the hand?
I am waiting, and the air crackles with the void. The
cold air seems to be against my skin all day, making
me feel unclothed. Where are your words? The mem-
ory of your eyes? Even your neck, drinking in the lux-
ury of turning for my lips, moving slowly in a dream
then, in a dream every night since then, your neck is
no longer moving. I am an animal lost on a windy night.

Tell me, my love, can we put this passion away
in a drawer, like a scarf that doesn't match this morn-
ing's suit? And if you would have me do that, then
what do I tell the fire in my chest, willing to send flames
into my hands so that they will reach out for you, touch
you in my dreams, touch me in reply? Shall I pretend
I can put out the fire? Stop thinking of your eyes, your
smile? You wouldn't ask me to do that, would you?
You are arriving, aren't you, my dearest Simone? Be
finally, committed.

Simone sent a telegram agreeing to meet at the band shell in Golden Gate Park. The day came and went. She hadn't made plane reservations. She sent a telegram the next day with no explanation, just an apology. She wrote another six letters filled with descriptions of kissing Meg, of the light in her flat at the moment that Meg climaxed. Finally, she sent a telegram agreeing to meet again at the band shell.

Flying from London to San Francisco, Simone bit her cuticles until they bled, then drank so many Bloody Marys that she fell asleep before the movie was shown. Dragging herself to the park, hung over, disheveled, she sat on a park bench underneath the truncated olive trees that dotted the sunken band shell.

Meg was on the other side of the band shell, in a feathered pillbox hat with a veil and a velvet coat, still a ghost. When she saw Simone she rose like a lady approaching the king, walking gracefully to her side. Simone thought of the warmth of Meg's lips, of the feel of her tongue running over Simone's collarbone. Of Benny Goodman music in the background.

Meg discretely slipped a gloved hand into Simone's.

"I'm so thrilled you've arrived. Come to my condo."

"Your what?" Simone stepped backward in shock.

"I want you to see where I live. I cook my lunches at the shop—and with you a few of my dinners—but you certainly didn't think I lived there, did you?" Meg laughed. "Come and meet my friends. I'm having a group over tonight to meet you, my darling."

Simone regarded Meg as a woman who had stuck her head through a cardboard cut-out of the era, as tourists do in Wild West towns when they have their photos taken in bustles and chaps. Meg had stepped from behind the cardboard, and Simone was bereft. She hailed a cab to the airport.

A week later, in London, she received Meg's last letter.

My dearest Simone,
I wanted you to know that there is beauty in the small
kiss. It is a kiss given in passing, in public, in airports,

before opening the door to my mother's house. It is dry-lipped, close-lipped. The tongue stays seated. It is not gripping or sweaty. There are no flailing arms or tangled legs associated with this kiss. It is tender because it knows the simple pain and fear of life every day, it knows the unspeakable sounds of early morning. To this tender kiss, laundry is loving.

I can hear you shrieking, Simone, but all those things you consider so pedestrian are, in fact, love and sex in the cups/mops/plates of two lives entwined. Can you see this, my beloved, whose fire leaps from paper? Not just legs wrapped or fingers engrossed in a message, but lives entwined. Admittedly, there are no delicious tastes or grateful sighs in picking linoleum, but afterward, every step becomes something shared, a thanksgiving, and when every step, every object is imbued with conviction and appreciation, they each carry their own little moan.

I saw a couple in their eighties yesterday and I stopped in the street to cry. They tottered on each other's arms, unable to walk apart any longer, and their clothes were so well-loved, scrubbed, pressed. Every inch of the two of them had been tended a thousand times by the other. Can you even imagine a passion that could burn not that bright but that long? I need to totter along with someone, Simone, to clutch a coffee grinder, just my setting, just my brand, more difficult to offer than lips on my breast.

My darling, Simone, my magician's explosion of

heat, I thank you for the burst of light that you have been, and through the puff of smoke I reluctantly give you up. The wider world of juice containers and mortgage payments calls me, offering dry kisses, passionate with a long, quiet history. I say good-bye. Be finally, alone.

imone flew into an icy pre-winter blizzard in Chicago, snarling at the gray snow and howling wind as she trudged down Michigan Avenue toward the Ritz. Love without sex, sex without love. Commitment to time, to place, to person. To hell with it all. And her with another damn envelope in her pocket. Lovers had left her wanting—one wanting to fill her cunt, and the other to fill her heart. She had arrived in Chicago a surly, confused, unloving woman trudging through a snowstorm. She imagined it wasn't a pretty picture.

The bellman put her luggage down carefully while Simone threw her leather rucksack on the bed and heaved the keys onto the table. She peeled off a bill and brusquely closed the door behind him. She grabbed the phone book and found the woman's listing right away, disdainful that it had been this easy, that there was no chase at all in this one. She placed a phone call.

"Elizabeth Staines, please," she said, bored, as she pulled off her boots and laid back on the bed.

"And whom shall I say is calling?"

"Simone Fitzwater." She was used to the name opening doors.

"One moment please."

"Hello?"

"Good afternoon, madam. I am Simone Fitzwater, granddaughter of Abigail Fitzwater, who is gravely ill."

"Yes?" the woman said, with as much boredom in her voice as Simone had when she began the conversation.

"I have a message for you or your mother. Perhaps your grandmother."

"Why on earth should I care about that?"

Simone sat up on the bed. "I beg your pardon?" Perhaps it was because of her grandmother's money, but she wasn't accustomed to being rebuffed.

"Oh, all right. I'm having people in at eight tonight. Black tie. You may join us," she said, and hung up the phone.

Simone scowled, then shrugged her shoulders. What did she care?

At seven forty-five, Simone stepped out of the cab in a crisp new tuxedo, her hair slicked back and knotted in a bun, her pants tailored, her black woolen coat hugging her shoulders and slapping against her legs. She lit a cigarette, though she hardly smoked, and flicked the match into the street. Simone felt tough and impenetrable as she blew the smoke out to mingle in the cold air. She looked up scornfully at the skyscraper that stood on the shore of Lake Michigan. A classic address, old money, and she didn't care if she shocked an intimate dinner of dowager Republicans with her boy-girlness. She was Simone Fitzwater.

"Staines," she announced to the doorman, who rang up, then escorted her to the elevator and pushed the button for the penthouse.

A butler opened the door for her, and she stood for a moment at the threshold. There were nearly one hundred people in the apartment, in gowns that had enough cloth for two, in suits, in gold, each clutching the thin stems of champagne glasses. Waiters in white jackets navigated through the crowd with silver trays. Old money all right, Simone thought, and decided it was definitely an evening for a whispered message and a quick departure.

Simone smelled caviar. She heard the piano in the background and watched the reflections of the candles and chandeliers in the big windows overlooking the lake. There was little to distinguish the party, the partyers, the apartment, she thought. People with money must all read the same magazines. She handed her coat and scarf to another manservant, waved away an offered glass, sought a pillar she could lean against until determining the target for her message.

She was folding her arms across her breasts, settling into her observation post, when a leg—lean, muscled, encased in black stockings, nearly disembodied—appeared at the top of a spiral staircase in the corner behind the piano. Simone drew her gaze up the sweep of the staircase and got caught on the hook of the black heel, the lack of a visible hemline. The leg was turned sideways, as if the woman attached to it were still conversing with someone on the upper floor, captured mid-sentence as she stepped. Simone wanted to run her lips up the tight, curving muscle to the woman's knee, slide around to the soft inside of her leg. She imagined sinking her teeth into the woman's thigh.

The woman descended, the short black skirt flouncing

around the tops of her thighs, lifting with the movement. Simone was going to have those legs around her. Pinning the woman to a bed, she would have them gripping the small of her back, flung over her shoulders as she dove. Those legs would be feeble and weak in the morning. She could feel the first moment of skin when she slipped her hands inside the tight elastic of the woman's panties and stockings. Her teeth hurt with it, her lips pursed at it. Simone wanted to break the skin and drink the woman's juice. This woman is mine, Simone thought, as she watched her move into the room.

Simone reached out and grabbed the woman's arm, pulled her toward her.

"Elizabeth Staines?"

"Staines *junior*," the woman sneered as a challenge, her lips inches from Simone's. She tugged against Simone's grip but seemed instantly locked into the combat, neither surprised nor daunted. Simone dropped her arm.

"Simone Fitzwater."

Staines cast a suspicious eye over Simone's face, then chortled. Simone's neck stiffened and her hands ached to grab the bitch's chin in her hand and kiss her right here in the middle of her party.

Staines gave Simone a tight little knowing smile. "This boring thing will be over by one," she said. "You can wait in the library if you like. We'll discuss your message then."

Simone paced nervously in the central reading room with its big leather chairs and green glass lamps. She tentatively opened a small door at the far end of the room. Low-wattage motion detector lights flicked on nearest the door, and a tiny row of lights, like runway markers, showed her the way into stacks. Simone was surprised to see such a cavernous space in an apartment. The area on either side of her was so dark that it was impossible to tell how big the room actually was, and after she ventured past the door, there were no lights other than the tiny markers. She put her hands in her trouser pockets and walked the length of the floor.

Metal shelves of books rose high above her head to the left and right. The floor was translucent glass about eight inches thick, catwalks a foot and a half wide with nothing on either side of them, framed by the metal bookshelves. Simone dipped her toe over the edge. She could see the faint outline of books on their shelves below. She couldn't hear the party, however, and had no idea where she was going. She slipped off her shoes, then her socks, feeling the cool glass on the balls of her feet. Quickly she unfastened her belt and slid her pants and panties into a pile on the glass floor. She looked to see if anyone was below her. The glass beneath her feet and the prospect of being seen from below brought the blood to her cunt. The runway lights left little gold spots on her ankles. Step by step, she walked along the glass catwalk, feeling the cold air rising against her labia, sensing invisible eyes through the floor staring up into her pussy. She stepped as if fearing the glass would break, although she could see it was thick. She took off her tie, her shirt, her bra, cupped her breasts in her hands, then presented them to the darkness, smiling at her solitude. She slowly prowled through the stacks, up stairs to higher floors, along narrow side rooms, happy to lose herself in this dark forest of books.

She willed Elizabeth Staines to come into the stacks. She summoned her forward. Finally, Simone heard the door open, saw the faint glimmer of the motion-detector lights on the floor below her. They were quickly extinguished. Simone froze where she was, her labia suddenly engorged. She heard the woman's heels click on the glass, then stop. Simone hurried toward the sound, knowing she was on the floor above her hostess. She glimpsed the smudge of the woman's black dress and flung herself against the floor, pressing her breasts against the glass and catching her hostess's upturned face, her expression of surprise. Elizabeth made no sound, not the gasp Simone expected nor the explicative that she was too cultured to allow herself. Simone arched her back and rolled her mound upward, then stood and disappeared into a side corridor. The room was absolutely silent.

Simone heard a few more clicking footsteps and stealthily tracked them with her eyes. She knelt on her forearms and her knees, pumping herself downward as she would when Elizabeth Staines wrapped her legs around her.

When Simone came down the stairs she found Elizabeth darting into the next aisle. She had lost her dress. Her silent, shadowy figure was bathed in white.

The women scurried up and down the floors, over the glass, playing cat and mouse until Simone looked up and saw Elizabeth lying flat on the glass, her legs seeming to go on for blocks, ending in a dark tangled mass of hair, a curve of hip, a navel, darkened nipples, face resting on a palm. Simone sprinted the stairs and flung herself on the outstretched woman, her skin glowing from the chase.

Elizabeth dug her nails into the back of Simone's neck and wrapped her legs around Simone's knees. She sneered at her, and Simone lunged forward, oblivious to the pain in her neck, grabbing Elizabeth's lips between her teeth. She sucked and bit, forcing her back onto the floor, where Elizabeth's head hit with a thud. Simone slid her big arms under the small of the woman's back and yanked her hips toward her. She pressed her mound into the woman's labia and ground on her.

She grabbed Elizabeth's nipples and squeezed in fury. Passion was only the chase, and here was a woman who loved being a cat. Elizabeth's nails drew blood from Simone's biceps but she arched her back and smiled. Simone slid down the length of her, feeling the woman's legs across her back and shoulders. Simone's nose slid through Elizabeth's hair, and while her tongue longed for her wetness, her teeth bit into the flesh of Elizabeth's thighs, held the skin in her mouth, sucking the blood to the surface. She wanted to shake the woman's thigh like a dog tearing meat off a bone. She wanted inside the sweet meat of the woman's legs. Simone bruised her while the woman moaned on the cool glass surface of her labyrinthian floors.

It may have been in the middle of the night, or perhaps the following morning—there was no telling in the catacomb of the library—when Simone retrieved their clothing and laid her jacket over the sleeping woman whose body was covered with bite marks. Elizabeth woke slowly, then pulled herself away from Simone.

"This is quite a place," Simone said.

"Elizabeth Senior's. My name is some humorous gesture on my mother's part to suggest that we actually had a connection."

She pulled on her dress without her underwear. "One thing she was very devoted to, though, was her books. Sent them from everywhere. There's three stories of them here."

"Who's the archivist?"

"I am," Elizabeth said with disdain. "I used to sit in here as a child and wait for her packages." She ran her finger along the spine of those nearest her, then turned away, pulled herself to standing. "Done up with strings and sealing wax medallions. Newspaper packing in languages that looked like magic. As you can see, of course, there are no children's books here. How could I have thought there might be something in all those boxes for me?"

Elizabeth pushed her finger against the leather spine of a book nearest to her and watched it fall three stories below. She pushed another backward until it fell as well.

"I hate her," Staines said under her breath.

Simone had waited herself. For the package, the postcard, the invitation, the plane ticket. Come hither. She had waited all her life for that. Little wonder seduction now seemed to be a viable lifestyle.

"Your mother and my grandmother probably traveled together," Simone said, buckling her pants but leaving her shirt open.

Elizabeth picked up a handful of books and hurled them down the catwalk, pushed her arm behind the shelf and knocked the entire contents onto the floor. She slowly walked through the stacks, leaving a trail of overturned books in her wake. Simone scrambled to her feet, grabbing the books closest to her. She turned and heaved them behind her.

What a price she had paid for her mother's passionate devotion to place, her choice of home over health. What a price for her mother's choice of men that eventually became a bargain costing her her life. How could she do it? How could she have sent Simone away and chosen a gin-swilling drunk instead? What a price she had paid for her grandmother's journey, for her hand-me-down life, a price she was still paying as she struggled to reconstruct a life that could have been hers.

Elizabeth and Simone, their clothing half undone, left socks, shoes, and lingerie under piles of books. They screamed and cried and overturned three stories of books into an indistinguishable mountain of bound paper. They climbed over the books as if they were rubble, then bringing their ferocious anger and searing pain with them, they fell onto the floor and devoured each other again.

For more than a month they lived in the stacks, sleeping curled on blankets in the corner, having food brought in on trays and clothing taken out in bags. Simone, who buttoned her shirt and snapped her pants for the first time in weeks, asked the butler to get her seventy-five postcards of Chicago, which she addressed to her grandmother and sent without any note attached. Let the absence of correspondence slap the old woman, make her take a moment to feel what it was like to receive a vacuous imitation of the love Simone should have gotten as a child. Let the old woman sit and stare at postcards in the night for a change, she thought furiously, and threw another shelf of books into a pile.

Simone and Elizabeth wandered amid the debris with half their clothes on, remorsefully bringing small piles of books to each other to sort and shelve. They fucked each other standing up, their backs pressed into the cold metal shelves; they fucked each other on the bare floor; they came pressed against the stacks of books. Their sex was angry. It bared its teeth and its fist and its snarl. The two women were longing and resentment in their thrashing sex. When they finished reshelving the first floor, they drank ouzo and tore it apart again. Time had no meaning. It was waiting, wishing, hating the void that remained. Elizabeth woke Simone three and four times a night to fuck her. She ambushed her several times a day.

One morning, Simone stood at a narrow window of the stacks, peering into the street at a pay phone by the lake's edge. Elizabeth wrapped one of her long legs around Simone and tried to turn her face. Simone pulled away. There was no filling the cavern of Elizabeth's second-hand mothering, no way to destroy the coveted books enough to make them lose their magical preference.

"Could you have the butler bring me a phone, please?"

"Why?"

"I'm going to ask her. I'm going to finally ask how she could make a choice like that. Leave a little girl in a boarding school for eight years when she had just lost her mother."

"And what do you think she's going to say?"

"Just get me the phone," Simone growled.

But Elizabeth was right. What did Simone expect her grandmother to say? How could the old woman manufacture a loving childhood for her at this late date? Worse yet, what if her grandmother didn't break down and apologize? What if she told her some other truth, something of children and boredom, of a child's unworthiness. The butler set the phone down in front of her and retreated.

"Come to me," Elizabeth said.

"No," Simone said irritably. She picked up the receiver. What if the fury rose in her and she was no longer able to chase the memories her grandmother needed? What if her grandmother revealed herself to be a woman so heartless that she was unworthy of Simone's devotion and Simone was left without anyone? If she abandoned her pursuit, she lost everything. Did she want to know the answer that badly?

Elizabeth started to cry and pulled on Simone's hand like a child. "Fuck them, we don't need them."

Simone stood rooted while Elizabeth tugged at her. "Elizabeth, is your mother alive?"

Elizabeth dropped her hand. "Yes," she said begrudgingly.

"How long has it been since you've spoken to her?"

"Four years. I don't have anything to say to her."

"How about 'I forgive you'?"

Elizabeth snorted at her, disgusted, and stormed off. Simone, herself, was surprised by the suggestion. More than her money and her penthouse, Elizabeth's anger was her entitlement. It had defined her personality, her view of the world and its workings.

"Who would be in charge, then?" Simone called after her, challenging herself as much as inciting Elizabeth. They were alter egos, weren't they? Both of them wallowing like toddlers in their own self-centered grief. Couldn't she say of herself, as much as she could say of Elizabeth, that they kept open the wound of childhood for their own gain? What would happen if Simone gave up the fury of her abandonment? Could there be a child's longing without a mother's sin?

Elizabeth whirled on her heels, picked up a book, and threw it at Simone. Simone dodged, then gathered her things and turned to go. As books began smashing on the walls beside her head, Simone opened the door into the blinding lakeside light and left.

When she arrived in Amsterdam, Simone felt as if she were visiting an old friend. She had begun to circle back, to revisit countries, slipping into the local sauna, lunching in the same square, calling on people she might someday be able to call friends. She had developed patterns of her own, preferences, and she felt a personal history start to build behind her shoulder blades. She had tromped these streets before and there was a safety in their familiarity. Ham, cheese, and bread on the *grachten,* the ice hanging from the gingerbread cornices of the old buildings, the haunt for fondue, another for brandy and chocolate milk.

Meeting women, she wanted to grab their shoulders and shake them, tell them what her grandmother had taught her through this journey: it mattered *how* you wanted passion and desire given to you. How *much* of it you wanted could run your life. Emotions are a wave—ride the ebb and flow or live a dry and barren life. You cannot hold back half the wave, plunging only into the lust and leaving the torment at the shore, embracing the joy without experiencing the silence. Simone couldn't know the truth of her grandmother's past without forgiving her. She couldn't be angry without risking everything. For now, Simone had decided that it was better to have half-knowledge than to risk it all.

In the women's bar, Sarraine, Simone walked away from women who slid next to her. She felt as if they had a drug in their touch that would pull her in as Elizabeth had. She didn't regard their bustlines or look into their eyes. Like a smoker counting the hours between cigarettes, Simone tallied the nights without sex as if proving to herself that she could say no. That she could turn away from passion, and perhaps even refuse her grandmother.

Waking with a clear head and a rested body, Simone took aerobic walks through the park, dropping to do push-ups and deep knee bends. Her body was her own. It was intact, inviolate, without demands or requirements being made of it by others. Her breasts felt tight, her cunt clean and contented.

She gathered another envelope, banked her money, delivered her message across town without ever taking off her coat.

The envelopes arrived in quiet succession. She made her plans methodically, boarded planes on time, navigated addresses, attended tea times and cocktail parties without incident. She drank no alcohol, smoked no cigarettes, slid into these women's lives and left again followed by the faint remembrance of the longing in their eyes, the frustration in their hands. Her libido was on hold, impervious to the seductive callings of the women around her. She wrote straightforward postcards to her grandmother, wrote copiously in the notebook which had become a family history journal.

One particularly equable night, a soft grey evening was draping the tight little houses on the *grachten,* women with string shopping bags walked easily home with children sweetly gripping their hands. Men were jocular and slow, each knowing their destination, intimate with every mortar, post, and pillar of their homes. It was the middle of the week, when the women in the bar were more apt to be talking motorcycles than sex, planning career strategies than trysts. Simone felt a wave of sadness welling up in her—she had nowhere to go, really, and she longed for the diffused light and intimate stillness of her home with her mother. She wanted a sofa that knew her imprint, a big cotton quilt, a potted plant, something special in the fridge. She could order it all up like room service, but it wouldn't be the same. She could pick a place, buy a house, but it still wouldn't be a home, not if she were to spend her time on the envelopes. And yet if she gave up her pursuit, where would she be? What would she do? An old ache burned behind her breasts, a longing for her mother's arms. For stillness. For home.

The next morning, an envelope arrived at general delivery and directed her across town. Simone was grateful she didn't have to check out of her hotel.

"What?" said a cranky voice, a cigarette making more of an entrance through the slit in the door than the face or the voice.

"Are you Sandra Weathers?"

"I am," said the smoker, opening the door just a bit.

"I'm the granddaughter of Abigail Fitzwater."

"Jesus." The door nearly closed. The cigarette popped through again, then Simone heard a heavy sigh.

"I'm looking for the Sandra Weathers who might have known my grandmother in…" Simone consulted her notebook. "In 1948."

"Am I supposed to be impressed? I can't believe it's taken all this time to get back here," the woman grumbled, abandoning the door and shuffling back into her apartment.

Simone stepped in behind her.

"I suppose I'm going to have to take my heart medicine to just look at you," she said with her back to Simone. She turned toward the young woman, shook her head and turned away. "If I had seen you from the window I would have thought senility was here for sure. Shit, you look just like her."

"I'm sorry to just arrive," Simone said, beginning her standard approach.

"Yes, it's terribly rude. I look like hell, the place is a mess. Goddamnit. Well, come in. Old ladies aren't supposed to refuse company. Shit."

The old woman tottered through the apartment toward her chair, using her cane to steady herself and pound on the floor for emphasis. She was wiry, dressed in faded peddle pushers and a cotton oxford shirt, broken-down Keds. Her hair was thin and short, but when she faced Simone, the young woman could see a bright fire in her eyes.

"And I don't have any decent bread in the house for lunch. I'm American, but I have it imported from England 'cause these Dutch pass off shoe leather for bread," the old woman said. "So, does she spend every goddamn waking moment on the phone with you, too?"

"I beg your pardon?"

"Her and her daughter! I spent three years of my life trying to break into the conversations between the two of them.

Sit down for chrissake! I'm in the middle of annotating a volume," she growled, stubbing out her cigarette and taking her place behind a long sloping editor's desk piled high with books and papers. "Of course, no one thinks the old have anything important to do."

What a delicacy, Simone thought—information on both her grandmother and her mother.

"Fitzwater, eh? I suppose you have more money than God."

"Yes," Simone said, refusing the chintz chair by the fireplace that was obviously the woman's concession to sociability. Simone settled instead in a hard wooden chair just like Sandra's on the other side of the desk. "Do you want some of it?"

"Yeah," Sandra said, fumbling for another cigarette. "I wouldn't mind some of it." She chuckled, softened. "And if you're a Fitzwater I'm sure you're damn generous with it. Orphanages and food banks all over town after the war with her name on them, of course."

"Would you tell me about my grandmother and mother?" Simone asked quietly.

Sandra blew the smoke out and dug between her teeth for tobacco. "Come back tomorrow, this time, and we'll have a chat. Now leave me alone so I can finish this," she said.

Simone stood. "She always loved you, Sandra."

"Funny, even after all these years I know that. Damn generous, you Fitzwaters."

The next day Simone arrived on time, wearing a pressed shirt and new trousers and holding a large basket of teas, fruits, and biscuits in one hand. She had a loaf of white Irish bread under her other arm. Sandra was neat and tidy in dark blue slacks and a pearl-buttoned blouse, the sleeves of which she rolled down and rebuttoned as Simone entered. The lights on the editor's table were glowing behind her, but today the chintz chair and its partner hosted a tea pot and cookies.

"She would lie there on the couch describing things to her daughter," Sandra said when the two had exchanged pleasantries and begun their afternoon. "She would send postcards from everywhere, three and four a day sometimes, and then she called every single day. Usually stretched out on a couch—here, in a hotel, didn't matter where—just blathering away. All about the steeples of this and the balustrades of that, the special way the bread crumbles, my God, yapping endlessly to that child.

"Your grandmother never spoke to hardly anyone else, including me, but that's all water under the bridge. You look surprised. You didn't know they talked?"

"I can honestly say that I have no memory of any phone call ever coming in from my grandmother," Simone said, astounded. "And no one I've met has mentioned this before."

"Well, now," Sandra said, shifting in her chair, "that's because you're visiting her...nighttime friends, shall we say. I was her friend. We traveled together, spent our days together. And she'd call during the day because you were away at school and your mother had no company. I got the feeling that all your mother ever did was lie around and talk to her own mother, and then sit around with you. Never heard about friends or company over."

"My mother never left the apartment. She was agoraphobic."

"Agoraphobic—is that what they called it?"

"I never saw my mother outside the apartment. Downstairs once or twice, but never in a park, or at my school, or outdoors at all."

"Well, she may have been afraid of *being* in the outside world, but certainly not of *knowing* about the outside world," Sandra said, pouring tea and lighting a cigarette.

Simone paced the room. In each of her previous visits, she had learned of a few operas her grandmother had attended, a charity ball, a vacation. Even when the woman she was visiting had clearly been deeply in love with her grandmother, there had been no mention of long-term friendship. Nor had she ever received news that was as startling as this. How was it that Sandra Weathers had wound up on the list to visit? Had her grandmother had lovers but no friends?

"Right over there," she motioned to the couch. "Talking with your mother for hours. The woman was Abigail's whole life. It was as if she considered it her duty to bring the world to her daughter. Go," she said, motioning again. "Lie down."

Simone ran her hands along the back of the sofa.

"Have you heard from my grandmother at all since those years?"

Sandra stubbed out her cigarette. "She'd stop in now and then. Your grandmother has always had a problem with consistency."

"If it's any consolation, three years seems to have been quite a long time for her," Simone said.

Sandra grinned a little. "Lovers need you. Friends just love you. Abigail only knew how to be needed."

Simone lay down on her side and closed her eyes. The best years of her life, she remembered, spent spooning with her mother while the sunshine struggled against the pull-down shades. To think of her grandmother, lying this way with the phone cradled in her hand, describing the world to her mother.

"My mother would whisper in my ear for hours," Simone said. "I thought they were things she had read."

"Descriptions of places?"

"Yes!"

"Your grandmother's travels. And mine, I might add," Sandra said. "Do you remember the packages?"

Simone shook her head. "I remember souvenirs."

Behind the sofa, at the far end of the living room in their apartment, her mother had kept a cupboard with a light burning inside. The slats of the louvered cupboard doors made the light spatter into the dark room with a halo effect. The glow was a constant, but Simone rarely saw its interior since her mother kept the cupboard closed until Simone was off to bed. The rare times that she padded into the room in her footed pajamas and her mother had the closet open were usually when she had a fever or couldn't sleep, and her mother would turn as if caught during a tryst. The cupboard held a built-in desk, and a bulletin board completely covered with what Simone now understood to be train and boat itineraries. Her mother, sometimes done up in formal wear, sometimes in an odd combination of her bathrobe and elbow-length gloves, would finger the bits of glass, tiny Limoge boxes, and the vast, jumbled assortment of expensive souvenirs that Nana had sent her.

Simone lay on the sofa and cried.

"The letters, do you remember the letters?" Sandra said softly.

"I was so young."

"Try to remember."

"I remember that my mother's middle finger was always blue."

"From the ink. Fountain pens. They wrote each other constantly. Frequently about you. I gathered these from upstairs," she said, pushing forward a big flowered storage box hiding between the sofa and the wall. "Who could have imagined it would have made it through the war but here they are. All those letters. Such goddamn devotion."

Simone rolled off the couch and dropped to her knees in front of the box but couldn't bear to open it. She couldn't quite bring herself to ask the question that tore at her. Sandra got up and poured two aperitif glasses of golden *jeunevier.*

"Some like their gin young but I prefer mine like brandy," Sandra said, placing the glass on top of the box.

"Why didn't she—"

"Your mother's remarriage was terrible," Sandra said. "A very bad choice on her part."

Simone dried her eyes.

"Of course he wouldn't stand for the phone calls. Had the phone removed at one point, I think."

"He sent me away to boarding school."

"Is that how it happened? I didn't think your grandmother had done that, and it certainly wasn't like your mother to send you away."

"I could never figure how he got her out of the house, into a car—"

"Terrible accident. I'm so sorry, my dear. Your grandmother was just destroyed by it. First the war, and then that. She went a little nuts, you know?"

"No. I never heard from anyone. Except postcards," Simone said with disdain.

"Ah, the postcards. She really was a little nuts."

"How could she have left me like that?" Simone blurted.

"Why don't you call her and ask her?"

"What could she possibly say?" Simone stood defiantly. "What reason could justify leaving me alone, an orphan?"

"Why don't you ask her?"

Simone thought of Elizabeth. "And do what, become furious and lose her too?"

"Is that what truth does, bring loss?"

"She isn't looking for a chance to listen to my anger."

"But she may be looking for a chance to explain. To apologize."

Sandra stood up, grabbed her cane, and walked around the room. "Sweetie, she couldn't sit still then. Couldn't seem to find anything to do, to absorb her. She flew everywhere, tried every cause under the sun. Inconsolable. And every time she had her head above water about the grief, she called for you. Do you know that? More than anyone, she had you brought to her. I couldn't take the wandering any more. I had to be someplace. Accomplish something—my cross to bear—so I came back and off she went. You should take those letters with you," Sandra said.

"If you don't mind, I'd rather leave them here," Simone said, standing and stepping back from the box.

"I'm pleased that that means you'll be returning, but I may be gone for a while," Sandra said.

"Where are you going?"

"To Boston, of course. Sounds like I have an old friend there who might need me." Sandra hit the box with her cane. "Pick the box up, dearie."

Simone was elated as she walked across Stephen's Green, the Dublin afternoon settling a fine mist on her cheeks. She had lain across the bed and on the floor of her hotel pouring over the letters. At first she had wept for lack of her mother, and then she had hungrily devoured the correspondence. Of course there were none of her grandmother's letters in the box so it was a one-sided view of life, but the one side Simone thought she'd never hear from again. Years of correspondence, several letters a day, describing in minute detail Simone's latest achievement, her growth, the funny things she said, her mother's response to Nana's adventures. Simone relived her childhood, revived memories, and basked in what she had previously been unsure of—her mother's connection to the outside world, her grandmother's attention to her mother. Simone kept a handful of letters stuffed in her pocket at all times and read them in restaurants, pubs, cafes, bookstores. As Meg had said about her correspondence with Simone, the letters had become her bones. They held Simone together now, made her taller, stronger, straighter. Her mother had been present, aware and cared for. Simone's mother had had a life with love, she said to herself with surprise—odd love, admittedly, but love nonetheless. There had been a caring and nurturing that she hadn't thought existed before, one that extended between generations and included herself.

Another envelope arrived before she had had time to write a letter or call her grandmother about the box of correspondence, but she happily boarded a train. Now she was a woman with a past. She went back to Italy, visited each of her previous lovers along the way, made the acquaintance of six new women whom she fucked in the dark, wet stillness of wine cellars, pressed against the chalky walls of the village bistro. Simone threw them into tall grasses on sloping hillsides, and thrust herself wildly into them in little modern apartments with paper-thin walls. She drove them out to the countryside and made love to them until she had to let them sleep in the back seat on the way home. She walked cobblestone streets with the smell of them deep between her fingers, their pubic hair caught between her teeth.

As the vaporetto rocked under her legs in Venice like a woman who knew what she wanted, Simone felt gloriously dangerous. Sex was a knife in her pocket. The lovers on this journey had taught her to use passion as a whip, snapping people to attention. She shook women out of their tightness, their lethargy, their refusal to abandon themselves to emotion. She showed them the self-cruelty of parceling out their feelings, their longings, their ambitions, their bodies. A woman stingy with emotion is a wicked sight, indeed. Simone had lain with an artist who had given up the chance for children to paint, then shredded her canvas in loneliness. She seduced a woman who had had her passion beaten out of her as a child, making her impervious to tenderness, miserly with food, touch, comfort, joy. Simone fucked a woman who refused her memories because there was bad with the good, a woman who lived hollowed out and emptied of her past. What you felt and what you desired—what you refused to feel and what you denied yourself—always had a price, whether you knew you were paying it or not.

Passion was dangerous, and she was the posse. The blood ran up her thighs, groping for the feel of muscled flesh between them. These days she had taken to wearing men's suits, tearing up the street with her stride, a rich, swaggering bulldagger. In and out of the leaning streets, she scoured the door fronts of a thousand Venetian lives, leaving a bit of her heat behind.

And what was the price that she was paying, Simone wondered, running her hands through her thick hair as if trying to discover who inhabited her head. The list had given her a purpose, but she still had no home, and her desire for place gnawed at her.

After several days of dead ends and bad leads, Simone found her next location. When she knocked she was instructed to sit down in the parlor of a bordello. Simone laid her head back, holding her pack—worn traveling companion. She smiled with ease: she could smell the women in the air.

She stood up to the counter, quickly made her way behind the curtain, greeted the women in lingerie as if she were their big brother.

Taking Simone by the arm, the grand lady, Cloe, strolled her through the establishment. They walked in on hookers on their bellies, their smooth round butts and fancy panties up in the air. In another room she saw them on their backs, their legs like branches of a healthy wild tree.

For days, Simone and Cloe lay across the stone bench in the garden, Simone sprawling on the woman as Cloe told stories of sex that made Simone's nipples hurt, the sunlight on her belly, her hands deep in the fly of her pants. Cloe unraveled a tale of every woman who had taught her technique. She remembered all of their names and just how their heads had moved when they had ridden her. Simone had the best moment of a Sunday afternoon, with the women in G-strings and thongs, satin bathrobes and torn T-shirts, the shower—full blast, full time—steaming up the corner of the building where glass doors opened to a garden and the women trooped in and out, dripping, singing, snapping towels, sharing soap. Simone lay down with them all, laughing her way through ouzo, cigarettes, pussy on her hand when she boarded a bus toward the market.

These women were a family to her, some connection with her elusive and sexual grandmother, her dead mother. Souls move around in pods, a learned lover had told her one morning with the sheets barely covering the tops of her wet thighs. The souls you meet now will be with you in another life, another manifestation, another relationship. These naked women were closer to the angels of her lineage than any other people in her orphaned world. To fuck them until they cried with release was to bond with them for life. Another branch of the family, these spirits, these naked women.

On a hot day when Simone sat in her own room of the

bordello in boxer shorts and a tank top, considering her pod and the women in it, Cloe arrived with a telegram.

Simone's grandmother had died. Abigail's will had specified that she was to be quickly cremated and scattered to the wind, without ceremony or memorial, and that bouquets of flowers be sent to her friends around the world.

Simone stormed through the bordello, furious that Phyllis and her grandmother's coterie hadn't waited for her return, hadn't included her in the last good-bye. Her fury was of the castaway child, though, and she lay weeping in a too-familiar stupor on the bordello floor. Just when she was piecing together her past. But even in the depths of her feelings of loss, in her sorrow for the end of her grandmother's life, she had to admit to herself that she was consumed with self-pity. She could see now that she had traveled the world this year not just to relay information to her grandmother, or even to chronicle the woman's life. She had actually believed that if she knew enough, gave enough, gathered enough, she could return to Boston and snuggle into the love and care of the old woman. She could be at home. Now there was no one to love her like a mother. No one she could accuse of neglecting their maternal duties. She had assumed that there was no way to fall any deeper into the feelings of neglect and abandonment than she had experienced as a child. The bottom had dropped out of even that deep pit of loneliness.

Cloe and the girls helped her into her bed, helped her through a few meals, gave her a long bath, moved her from room to room to sleep in their arms. Perhaps worse, Simone explained, was the feeling of her grandmother being scattered, adrift during her life and dispersed in death.

A huge bouquet of flowers arrived for Simone. She envisioned thousands of bouquets of flowers being sent all over the world, following not only her grandmother's footsteps but her own. She imagined that flowers were landing on doorsteps she hadn't yet visited, comforting women she hadn't yet met. She pulled the flowers from the bouquet and, one by one, burst into the rooms of the bordello, handing them over the sweaty shoulders of men to her friends.

Ensuing documents explained that her grandmother's money was now legally hers, without stipulation—far more money than Simone had thought. She could settle in somewhere and never move again. No more passport, money, envelopes. She could give up this life offered by her grandmother. However, her nana's will decreed that the envelopes would be sent as usual if Simone chose to continue the journey. Phyllis reminded her that she still had one name outstanding. Simone, numb with grief, cast adrift, sent a telegram asking for time to make her decision.

*I*n Barcelona, the long boulevard smelled of chestnuts as Simone flopped onto a bench, exasperated. She had been winding through the narrow, cobbled streets, crossing the Ramblas with its gnarled leafless trees and newspaper stands, following what she thought was the route to the Calle de Cabarello, only to discover that she was being led by the smell of fried squid. Cabs did not run through the Gothic Quarter so there was no way to put herself in someone else's hands. Every time she asked directions she was sent on a twisted course, different from the last and equally unsuccessful. She had looked all day yesterday to no avail, and today it seemed she would fail as well.

She turned into a market, the tin roof reverberating with the shouts of women calling for a kilo of oranges, a better price for chicken.

Embarrassed that all she could utter was a crude *¿donde es?,* Simone held up her slip of paper into the women's harried and sweating faces. They pinched the note between their oil-stained fingers, then waved her on.

Finally, a woman behind a stall of pistachios grabbed her by the wrist.

"Abigail!" she shouted, then tossed Simone's wrist away. She frantically consulted with a woman in a shapeless black dress and a black shawl.

Simone cleared her throat and bowed her head nervously as the woman looked up at Simone and raised her eyebrows. Simone attempted a smile. The black-garbed woman disappeared into the crowd and Simone quickly followed her as she walked through a labyrinth of narrow streets made dark by the three stories of shuttered old buildings and heavy wooden doors.

The woman in black opened a small door set into a large set of double oak doors studded with black iron hinges and pegs. Simone bent low to enter and stood in a courtyard covered with old vegetation and large clay pots. The woman motioned her to a bench, which Simone sat on with her rucksack in her lap. She watched the fall of water in a large fountain in the middle of the courtyard. Suddenly, a young woman in a mint-green sundress appeared, grabbed Simone's hand, and pulled her down a corridor off the courtyard. She led Simone into a room and shut the door.

The woman stood three feet in front of her, her eyes bright and her full lips pressed against laughter that tensed her jaw. Her hair was an inch long, laying like a thin piece of silk on her scull. She was as thin as a reed with huge dark eyes.

"Abigail Fitzwater—" Simone began, but the young woman laughed again, pressed her palms together.

"Yes, yes," she said with a thick Spanish accent. "I saw you there, I thought, the Fitzwater vagabond! Your family is legendary in my family, but I thought—so serious! This woman needs some fun. Plenty of time for my grandmama, yes?"

"Yes," Simone said emphatically.

The woman smiled and reached for a white shawl hanging on a peg. Her perfume warmed in Simone's nostrils. The woman, Anya, took her to cafes where the squid was pulled steaming of sea and garlic from ovens in the stone walls, then to bars where they held double-spouted glass decanters into the air to pour its red wine down their throats. They ate pastries at street-side cantinas made of old gypsy wagons, holding hands under the chest-high counter. At dawn, they were the first customers to nestle into chairs at the long marble tables of a cafe where hundreds of canaries chirped from cages on the walls.

Exhausted, they crept into the back door of Anya's house and into her bed, where Simone kissed the down on her belly and the crest of her hipbones as if Anya had saved her, released her from her task. This could be her last destination. She could be someone other than a Fitzwater vagabond.

Simone burned the taste of the woman's sex into her mind as something precious and private. She grasped Anya's ankles and ran her hands fiercely up her legs, trying to remember, to possess, to prove something to herself. After Anya had climaxed, arching her back off the sheets and digging her nails into the bedposts, it was Simone's tears that collected in a puddle in the soft dip of Anya's collarbone.

"You'll be my last, Anya," Simone said at noon the following day, struggling into her clothes.

But Anya put a firm hand on her back and pushed her out the back door. "You are expected now."

Anya's grandmother greeted Simone in the courtyard and

ordered that tea and bread be brought to the long iron table under the largest tree. The old woman was entirely swathed in brown, her tiny veined hands and a small lined face peeking from the dress, shawl, and a brown lace mantilla that cascaded onto the courtyard tiles. She asked Simone to pass a plate of pastries sitting within the woman's grasp. Her eyes were unchanging as Simone rose, came to her end of the table, and lifted the plate to a spot inches from her face. Simone bent forward slightly in surprise, leaned from side to side, and then realized the woman was blind.

"Oh," Simone said shamefully, setting the plate of pastries into the woman's hands. "I'm very sorry."

"I don't see well anymore," the old woman said. "Anya insists that I tell people, but it is one of the last vanities I have. That and...," she said, removing the mantle of lace, "dying my hair. Is it lovely?" The lustrous brown mane of hair, nearly the color of her dress, curled from her crown to her shoulders.

Simone's eye was caught by a movement upstairs on the balcony above the courtyard. At first she thought it was a curtain blowing in the breeze, but then she had a glimpse of Anya, walking through the room in a short vest that barely covered her small, tight breasts, her bare thighs and brown ass moving languidly.

Simone instinctively looked back at the grandmother to see if the woman had noticed her longing gaze, then slyly looked up at the balcony again, where Anya had walked outside and was now leaning on the wrought-iron railing.

She cupped her breasts in her hands, the black vest gathering under her soft arms. She turned her head from side to side as she kneaded her breasts and squeezed her nipples. Simone gripped her tea cup. Anya leaned against the railing, her eyes closed and her nipples tight in the grip of her fingers. She slung her leg around a wrought-iron pole and pressed her breasts against either side of the cool metal, then moved across the balcony and slipped into another room.

"Madam," Simone said, wishing to fulfill her task, "my grandmother has sent me..."

"That is a conversation for sherry and fruit," the woman said. "Anya!" she called in a reedy voice. The young woman slowly descended the courtyard stairs, still in her vest, her triangle of black hair gleaming in the sun, her olive skin radiant.

"Time for a delicious meal, grandma, yes? I've sent the maid home and I'll fix you your favorite," she said, her eyes riveted on Simone.

"Yes," Simone said, her skin prickling with the danger of Anya's nakedness and her own part in the charade. "Madam, I have been sent—"

"I won't hear a word of it," the woman said sternly. "You must enjoy your dinner. Then you may deliver your message. Allow an old woman to control what little she can."

Anya had slipped a knee-length apron over her vest, leaving it untied so it swung over each of her hips, exposing her muff as she walked. She delivered a bounty of food while facing her grandmother, leaning far over the table at Simone's elbow until her body lay nearly horizontal along its length. Her tight brown buttocks greeted Simone as she set down bowls of wrinkled black olives, heads of garlic fried in olive oil, moist red pimentos striped black from the searing pan. Simone's mouth opened, instinctively. Anya continued until the table was almost covered with pungent, steaming foodstuffs barely contained in their plates and bowls. Her grandmother, without seeing the contents, brought each to her face, groped for the spoon wedged among the morsels, and filled her plate, smiling.

Simone reached for eggplant dotted with sun-dried tomatoes. She gasped. Hands gripped her ankles, moved quickly up to her thighs. Anya had slipped under the table, and was grasping the edge of her panties. Pushing her fingers into Simone's ass, Anya stripped them off her and lay her warm lips on Simone's thighs.

"You must have some of the olives," the grandmother said as a shiver ran along Simone's spine.

"It's delicious," Simone said nervously, picking up her fork. She brought the eggplant to her lips. Anya brought her lips to Simone. In Simone's mouth, the taste of the rich food mingled with the heat rising through her body, the texture of the pungent, oily dinner with the feel of Anya's tongue. She struggled to breathe into her excitement and spoon food into her mouth. She bit into her fork, gripped her wine glass.

Each time she stopped for breath, to drop her fork and seize the edge of her chair, Anya stopped.

"Eat your dinner," the old woman admonished. "I can't hear you eating."

Simone panted, surveyed the table to see what delight she hadn't savored. She carefully lifted herself from her chair, stretching to reach a platter. Anya thrust her fingers deep inside Simone and she collapsed into her chair, fighting the pounding desire to let out a moan that would make the birds lift from the tree above them.

"Yes, of course you enjoy my beautiful meal," the old woman said.

Simone slunk lower into her chair, slipping a bit of fruit compote into her mouth, gliding it along her teeth as Anya moved her fingers deeper inside and lowered her lips to Simone's sex again.

"And now," the old woman said, "I'll leave you girls to your dessert."

Simone's eyes widened. She blushed wildly, her vulva clutching at Anya's presence. The old woman rose, and groping for the edge of the table to get her bearings, stepped with great caution toward the open door of the library.

Simone and Anya joined the old woman later. She was standing at a huge fireplace whose mantel held scores of photographs. The old woman fingered the petals of a flower bouquet sent from the Fitzwater estate. Simone resisted the urge to search for her grandmother's face among the pictures.

"Grandma," Anya said. "Simone is thinking of giving up her journey. No more Fitzwater vagabond, she says."

"I'd like to deliver a message from my grandmother," Simone said defensively.

The old woman was very quiet, then picked up a frame whose contents she couldn't see, and turned.

"You need to take this journey very seriously," she said. "You see, there are some women born into the world for small

passions. They marry. They dig and scratch for little bits of love."
She ran her hand along the edges of a frame. "A dog, perhaps.
A rose bush. If they are lucky, a daughter. But women like your
grandmother and you, my dear, are born for big love. Love that
gives the world its humid smell." She laughed. "The Fitzwater duty is to sweat into the rivers, little Simone, to be fire on
a hillside. Live it, grasp it in both hands and hold it tight against
your lips. Do it for the rest of us poor, pitiful things, who scram-
ble for love that is no deeper than the lick of a selfish cat. Continue your journey for those of us who can only stay at
home and dream of your adventures."

Simone stood very quietly for a moment, then walked to
the old woman and kissed her on her soft lips.

"She always loved you."

Simone returned to Anya's side, grasping her soft shoulders. "Come with me," she whispered.

"No," Anya said, shaking her head as she gestured to her
grandmother.

Simone pressed her cheek in pain against Anya's, stepped
away. A solitary journey? Was she to be relegated to the love
of many but never of one?

"Anya," she pleaded, but when Anya sadly shook her
head again, Simone turned, clenched her teeth, and headed
toward the train station.

Simone sat in the rarefied nighttime of the transcontinental airplane. She was on her way to Thailand and was glad she was still airborne. She had lost a sense of where she was going or why, moving without a destination that was not completely chartered by the manila envelopes pressed inside her passport. She was a pawn in someone else's game.

It seemed to Simone that her body was a device for moving her head around as she thought about envelopes and urns of ash, no longer conjuring images of breasts and thighs and the white heat that used to rise through her. Place or purpose. For Simone, they were two opposing passions insisting that she choose. Now that her grandmother was dead, the purpose of her travels had taken on a new light. She had electrified women to help them bring passion into their lives; she had tromped the globe to describe the world to her dying grandmother. The old woman in Barcelona had begged her to continue for the women who lived with small loves. But what was she doing for herself? Without her grandmother, she felt unwanted, unneeded.

In a Bangkok marketplace, Simone drank a tall glass of thick orange tea. The noon heat crowded around her, making her feel even more limp and directionless. The women in the marketplace fanned themselves slower, putting up sun umbrellas and finally producing bits of fish and rice to eat when their customers refused to venture into the heat. Simone felt the sweat collecting around her breasts, dripping down her cleavage, while the humidity soaked her white shirt until it was almost transparent.

The envelope directed her to Mai Roongruang, whose address was at the top of a chrome and glass skyscraper in Bangkok. After locating the apartment, Simone had to pass through several groups of relatives who left their televisions to inspect a lone white woman coming to see their grandmother. When Simone reached her, the tiny, wrinkled old woman had just heard of her arrival and was struggling to get out of her chair, rearrange her bright silken shawls, and totter to Simone's side with her cane. A granddaughter brought Mai her glasses, which Mai put on and peered upward into Simone's face. She smiled and stomped the floor gleefully with her cane. Simone, unable to return her smile, bowed at the waist to the old woman.

"My grandmother, Abigail Fitzwater, has a message for you," Simone said gravely.

Mai took Simone's hand and placed it on the top of her cane, sandwiched in between her gnarled hands. "I received the flowers," Mai said. "I'm very sorry for your loss."

Simone felt herself descending into a place of grey light, unable to move or respond. Mai pulled her shawl around her and requested that the granddaughter bring her her purse. "I owe your family much," she said. "I take you on a journey now."

Mai took Simone's arm and admonished the relatives who jumped in front of her, pulled on her, and shrieked their alarm to prevent her from leaving. The two managed to get into the elevator. Mai pushed the last grandson out of the way with her cane just before the doors closed.

"My grandchildren know more about Hollywood than they do of the debts of their grandmother," Mai said. "Abigail Fitzwater gave me the money to start my business. And now I have enough to keep my grandchildren around me—and live out my last years as their captive. This is the condition of their love."

Mai hailed a taxi and took Simone to a pier. Four thin boats, bright yellow with wooden canopies and flowers hanging off their dragon-face prows, bobbed beside them.

"Grief has taken your heart?" Mai asked the silent Simone as she watched the boats.

"My direction," Simone said. "I've lost the connection. I've lost the feeling, the purpose. I was going to give up my journey in Barcelona…"

"But some old woman begged you not to," Mai said, taking Simone's arm and smiling. "Your grandmother was a magician. I imagine it's a demanding job."

Simone held Mai's hand against her ribcage and longed for Jana Stor, for her directives and orchestration.

"Tell me what to do," Simone asked Mai.

The old woman patted her arm and guided her into one of the dragon-prow boats. She took Simone to a hotel that bordered the river and checked her into a room jutting out on a pier over the water. Pushing Simone into the room as if she were a reluctant child, she closed the door and left her. Moments later, a young woman who introduced herself as Nid came into the room and inspected the corners of the sheets for insects. Simone squatted over the seatless toilet, then threw a small pan of water from an open cistern down the commode. The hotel was built on stilts. Simone saw the piss and the water fall directly into the mud below her.

Nid first fussed in the room before turning her attention to Simone. She stripped her clothes off while Simone stood as if in a trance. She pulled a chair into the center of the room, directly in front of the door, and sat Simone on it.

The young Thai woman unrolled a canopy of mosquito netting, hooked it to the ceiling, and made a small tent over Simone's nakedness. She muttered in Thai and opened the door so Simone could stare out at the winding river, a shimmering temple, and old teak boats. Nid sat on an end table and crumbled Thai-stick into a small pipe, then filled the room with the pungent smell. She ran hot water into a large pan, brought the pipe, the pan, a rough sponge, and a small stool to Simone's tent. Nid lifted the netting and moved her stool behind the exhausted traveler, put the pipe into Simone's mouth and scrubbed her back with the hot water and the sponge. She soaked hot towels in mint water and wrapped them around Simone's shoulders, hid her hair within a turban of white towel, and beat the tired muscles of her back with the loofa.

Nid tied her skirt up around one hip and rode Simone's leg as she massaged her neck muscles. The soft skin of Nid's upper thighs and the tickle of her pubic hair should have brought Simone to her senses, should have made her reach out and cup Nid's buttocks with her hands, bring the woman's leg up to her own cunt. Instead, she sat motionless, only tipping her head from one side to the other as Nid worked. The smoke circled around them, trapped inside the fine mosquito netting. Outside, the Bangkok sunset made the golden temple glow.

Nid retreated to her stool and brusquely grabbed Simone's breasts. Pulling Simone between her legs and squeezing her nipples, Nid massaged her breasts as she bit into the fleshy spot between Simone's shoulder blades and neck. She moved her hand over Simone's long abdomen, then got up to retrieve a small bag. She sat down on the stool again, reloaded the pipe, and as the dense smoke swirled, pulled out a dildo that she sheathed and slid into Simone's unsuspecting cunt. Simone's breathing deepened. Encouraged, Nid first began to tease the dildo back and forth, then changed her mind and abandoned it inside Simone's pussy. She pulled a rope out of her bag and, standing on her stool so that the coarse hair of her crotch grazed Simone's turban and her smell filled Simone's nostrils, she tied Simone's hands together and threw the rope over the ceiling struts for the mosquito netting.

For the next several hours (or was it days? Simone couldn't tell), she sat on her stool with her arms above her head as her Thai friend hung beads from clips pinching her nipples, circled her, then added shiny chains to the beads. As the night air wafted in the open door, she added weights to the chains, talismans in the shape of golden pomegranates and flowers. The pain in Simone's nipples was a luscious sting that made her dream of needles shooting out from her areola. Every time the woman clipped a brass monkey or a copper bird onto the chain, Simone closed her eyes and let her head fall backward.

Soon, the tearing sensation in her nipples had her panting, the perspiration gathering on her top lip.

Simone rode the stool, pressing on the dildo while the chains jingled with her efforts. Boats passed the open door with their running lights on, shining skeletons of ships. Still there was no connection between the white hot pain in her nipples and her mind. Nid crossed her arms in front of her chest and stared at her with determined, dark brown eyes. It was clear that other measures would be required, she explained in halting English.

Nid cut Simone down, rolled her in stiff linen sheets, and laid her on the hard, narrow bed to sleep. In the morning, Simone opened her eyes to see Nid bringing in tea on a small flowered tray, and beyond her, the bright choppy water of the Bangkok Noi. Mai stood behind her, leaning on her cane.

"Your grandmother was fond of dancing," Mai said. "I will show you one of her favorites."

The three women sat shoulder to shoulder in the narrow boat as its dragon prow rose above the water. They turned into the maze of cramped backwater canals where the houses rose on stilts on each side of the boat, the floorboards high above the passengers' heads. The teak floors of the houses gleamed with moisture. The humid air plastered Simone's shirt to her breasts.

The boat pulled up to a low, undulating dock as passengers rearranged their parcels, passed back a few silver coins, and clambered onto the rough planks. Mai, Simone, and Nid were the last to disembark, stopping in front of a brown teak house with an upturned roof.

Mai spoke to a man who greeted them while Nid escorted

Simone into a small room with no furniture where one entire wall was latticework. Simone sat limply on the floor. An hour later, Nid came in once again and stripped Simone of her clothing, then left without speaking. Simone felt like a hollow gourd. She stared, motionless, at the pinpoints of water that twinkled through the lattice. Evening began to descend, the light grew pale, and Simone heard snatches of music made by stringed instruments and drums. Nid reentered and turned Simone toward the door, handing her a goblet of sweet, drugged tea, leaving the door open when she departed. By the time the goblet was drained, there was a soft haze around the edges of Simone's eyesight. Candlelight flickered in the hallway; the sound of drums rose around her. People were amassing outside the door but she sat very still, unconcerned with her nakedness.

It began to rain, the water pouring down the sides of the building. Simone saw it coming down in sheets beyond the hallway, heard it splashing off the eaves on the other side of the latticework. The rain closed them in, rinsed the inside of her.

Two women entered the room and laid grasses around her. Two others came in and poured scented water over her shoulders. Another pair stood her up and slipped thin shoes on her feet. A final set draped her shoulders with a bright cape. The drums pounded outside the room. The women took her by her passive arms and led her into the hallway, where she stood in front of two dozen people, the cape straight down her back, the rest of her naked to the assembled group. Her nakedness made her feel as if the rain were pelting her skin.

They walked her to a long table on the balcony of the house, with the rain pouring in a grey sheet beyond the ceiling and the candles dancing around her. They laid her out on a table. Simone felt the drums pounding against her belly and the strings vibrating against her nipples. Her mind fell into a blur of drugs and rain and candles and she was aware of being carried on a pallet around the balcony. First with leaves and palm fronds brushing her chest and belly, then with flowers, then with the hands of what seemed like scores of people touching her as she passed, lying immobilized on her pallet. They draped her with beads, they laid berries and nuts on her flat belly, they pushed flowers into the crevice between her torso and arms.

They set the pallet down on the table again and circled her with the candles. Two dozen hands slipped underneath her. As she closed her eyes, they lifted her up, set her down again, slipped hands under her buttocks and lifted her once more. She couldn't make out faces, couldn't distinguish genders, but she heard the voice of Mai in the distance. The music seemed to be on all sides of her, to have entered her. Now, in a fevered pitch, the drums called each of the throng to climb onto the table and lie on her, to rub their cool flesh against her, some hard between the legs and some not, some soft in the chest and some not. They kissed her, they entangled her legs, they lightly grazed her skin and dismounted, they pushed themselves firmly into her chest and hips. There were so many people that they blurred into a shifting, morphing mass of flesh and tenderness. Simone had been robbed of her mind, and since her will had already deserted her, she was only a body, flesh that was vibrating like the stringed instruments and drums playing around her.

Taking the dragon-prow boat back to her hotel late that night, Mai at her side, Simone experienced every tiny light along the canal as the candles around her body. She felt herself attached in some way to each of the people who had pressed little bits of their sexuality into her. To rejuvenate her, to continue the conversation begun by Anya's grandmother in Barcelona. There was a thread running from her to Mai, to the group in the rain, to the dancers and Jana in Stockholm, to Anna's studio in London, to Cloe and the wild labyrinth of women she had visited all over the world.

Sex was a gift that connected them, not just each to the other, but each to the previous generation and the stories they told, the fears they instilled, the secrets they shared that their daughters might grow up to know passion and pleasure. It was a strong thread, invisible, spanning time and geography. Simone again knew herself as the point of its needle, refocused in her pursuit. Weaving in and out of the world of women was her life and her luxury. She kissed the old woman's hand in gratitude, helping her into a cab.

Even if she were no longer required to follow the meanderings of the envelopes, she knew now that she would continue. The envelopes were all Simone had, her passport sitting stiff against her breasts in her cotton traveling pouch. It was filled with brightly colored stamps and evidence of her journey, more like a family album than any she had had. The letters, her sketchy, inaccurate journal, and her passport.

Simone's pursuit had become one extending beyond history and family. She was more than a messenger. She was a sexual catalyst who had altered these women's lives, as her grandmother had done. She was the reminder that sex and freedom and boundless pleasure still existed in the world, a lightning rod drawing a sexual current and spreading it through the earth. This was her task. She was good at it, too, and as the old woman in Barcelona had made it clear, someone needed to be good at it. In return, Simone's lovers had defined her. Their textures had painted themselves on her, an invisible etching on her skin. Their bodies, stories, pasts, requests had given her a vision, a proclivity. They had defined her life.

But the price of her purpose was the loss of her place. Home was not to be an option for her. If she returned to her grandmother's house in Boston, she would simply become a chronicler of objects, finding the stories behind this vase or that marble egg, putting the letters in perfect order. But Simone knew that passion was not tidy or predictable. Safely ensconced in her Boston mansion she would lose the chase, the seduction, the discovery. She would lose the chance to get lost, chartless in the cities, chartless in love. Every day she stayed put was a day she failed her purpose.

She wrote a postcard to Phyllis: *Passion is our obligation, as life demands its verve.* It was time to find a boat schedule, a timetable for the plane.

*I*n her Dublin hotel room, Simone stood naked in front of the mirror, her labia swollen and moist, her nipples purple and erect. Perhaps she had never wanted a woman as badly, nor had she ever been rejected as soundly as she had by the diva that night.

The singer had been in electric blue like the whirling dancer in Stockholm, and sitting in the opera house, Simone had felt her own buttocks wanting to lift into the air and receive this artist. The woman strode among the milkmaids and soldiers, the music pouring from her throat, emanating from her hands. Her hair was twisted into snakelike coils behind her head, and her heavily made-up eyes were beckoning and hungry. The woman's breasts radiated with a heaving, dewy white translucence that made Simone's own breath rise and fall. Each cresting wave of song brought life into the woman's breasts, made them threaten to emerge from the deeply cut neckline of her electric blue dress, made Simone, mesmerized, lean on the railing of her private box. The woman strode across the stage, raising a bejeweled hand to the sky, her voice filling the hall. Simone saw the patch of skin she wanted for her own, the glittering fingers she imagined running across her hips. Throughout her travels and seductions, many of the others had come to her easily, floating into her lap and her pants. This one was all pursuit.

Simone lit the candles in front of the glossy photos of the diva. She smoothed her hands over the program. To touch the diva's skin was impossible, but to live the sensation of the woman's breasts against her breasts, against her cheek, gliding softly across her belly, held tightly within her lips, this was possible as she stood here in the candlelight, her hands cupping her own breasts. The scissoring legs that had carried the diva across the stage could wrap around her, even though the woman was miles away, Simone thought, as she fell to her knees and ran her hands across her rib cage. These were the diva's hands—tugging on her pubic hair, pulling her labia open, making her feel the cool night air against her clitoris. She bowed to the pictures, then moved the first fingers of both hands into her cunt, her thumbs massaging her clitoris. She devoted one of her hands to her clitoris, the other to exploring the tightly ribbed depths of her body.

Through all the miles and all the lovers, this one would consume her, she thought, feeling the intoxication move up her body. This love had stolen a part of her because the diva would give nothing, and so she became the definition of everything, the essence of exquisite, of soft. When not returned, longing achieves an unaltered perfection.

Simone's nipples ached for the feeling of the diva's teeth. Her hot cheek pressed against the cold floor as her fingers sped through a dance on her clit. As her fingers probed so deeply inside herself that she felt the rain pour out in a pulsing rhythm, Simone knew the diva would be an exquisite torture.

Simone took buses across America, sexual soldier to the envelopes. At a commune in California she walked through the musky earth of the fruit orchards after an old wooden slat truck. The women climbed ladders and let the afternoon breeze lift their skirts above their bare butts. Simone threw a bucket of sun-warmed water over her head, squeezed her own nipples until she flinched, and climbed the ladders behind them. A woman flung a leg over Simone's shoulder, laid back along the slatted ladder, and came hard, her lips to the sun. They fucked in the fruit trees, the smell of ripe oranges around them, the wet peat of the earth underneath. Simone climbed ladder after ladder, and carried her baskets of fruit to the trucks.

She boarded a train to New Orleans, met girls on the street near the French Market, slept in old cars with fins by the side of a creek bed, the corn up higher than the car, their feet out the window, their knees against the back of the car seat.

She scoured the earth with her lips, biting the heads off shellfish and lawn shrimp, devouring cobs of corn as if they were the flesh of her woman's thighs. She was a carnival hustler, swaggering in the Louisiana heat. She pounded into a girl while riding down the freeway in the back of a flatbed truck.

Another envelope, another plane. Abigail's life, her own life, Abigail's past and her own mingled, crossed, separated, and Simone emerged as her own woman, carrying on the line. She trudged sideways on an Alpine mountainside, bringing bread, honey, coffee, and cheese to a shepherd and her flock. Simone and her new-found friend rocked their spines in the shade of a tree, her knees open and blessed by the sun, her pussy taking in Simone fast and hard. Every day Simone came to the grassy knoll and stripped off her clothes, rode the woman like a raucous goat, licked the lunch crumbs off her cheeks, and sent her off to work again. Day after day, balling and rocking, falling asleep in the shade of the tree, Simone's pussy was with the lunch pouch, sent to revitalize the shepherd.

Journeys that had taken days now took years. She was in love a thousand times, pledged a thousand nights and delivered a hundred days. She was shameless in her seductions and her troth each time she raised her arm to knock on a new door, her hardened nipples her calling cards. She fell in love and tore her own heart apart. There were women with children who considered her family, there were seaside, lakeside, mountaintop trysts, comfortable lovers who turned into friends. Her passionate longing for her mother and a home would be a pain that traveled every step with her, but it was a burr in her side that she was unwilling to remove.

*W*hen Simone awoke, forty years later, she gazed up at the soft white linen of her grandmother's canopy bed, her own snowy hair fanned out on the pillow. She could feel the train pulling out of the station without her and could hardly imagine that her body was still.

"Phyllis?" she said sleepily.

"No. Gretchen," said a woman as she came to the bedside and laid a small hand on Simone's arm. Wrenlike, as Phyllis had been, this handmaiden had salt-and-pepper hair and sported multicolored square glasses. "Her successor, so to speak. Keeper of your list."

"You've been here?"

"All these years. Directing. Well," she lowered her voice and adjusted her glasses, "devoted to you, actually. Trying to anticipate whom you might need next. Your job was to journey and mine was to stay here and prepare for your arrival."

"Devoted to me?"

"All this time." Gretchen smiled sheepishly like a mail-order bride. "The marvelous news is that I think we've found someone in your lineage to carry on your task. She brought you home from the train station." Gretchen positioned the pillows and helped Simone sit up. She motioned to the corner of the room and the young woman with black hair stood and approached the bed.

"Granddaughter of your father's niece. Judith Fitzwater."

Simone, still startled by the resemblance between the two of them, closed her eyes in relief that the girl was not an apparition as she had thought at the train station. The girl was not time's messenger, sent to collect her and propel her back, yet again, on her wonderful, exhausting journey. Simone struggled to get out of bed despite Gretchen's timid protests, and she tottered over to Judith, who remained impassively still. Simone looked into her eyes, took her by the arm, and lead her to a vanity mirror. She regarded the two of them side by side and smiled for herself. The bitter hunger that she had had in her eyes at Judith's age was gone. Beyond the crow's feet, the chicken-skin eyelids, and the fatigue, it was clear that her eyes were warm and full, that she had won her battle with a past of desertion.

Simone looked at young Judith, so fresh and beautiful and angry, and put her arm around the girl, pulled her in tightly as if in a headlock, and covered the girl's eyes with her hand just to stop their burning intensity for an instant. It would be impossible to tell her that there were enough breasts and thighs and vulnerabilities in the world to mend the wound, that if she were paying attention there were lessons on the journey on how to fill up the abyss of her loneliness. There was no telling where, or with whom, of course. The kindest thing Simone could do was simply to make the journey possible.

"They will beg to smell the color of your hair, my dear," Simone said, patting the girl's arm and returning to her bed.

"Judith, would you see about tea?" Judith nodded curtly and left the room.

"Care to begin a list for her?" Gretchen asked. "As I understand it, your lovers only. That is, no one from the previous list."

Simone smiled. Gretchen sat with her pen poised on the paper. "We have to leave our money to someone," she said. "And then our time is ours."

"Together?" Simone asked.

"If you like."

"The descendants of Jana Stor in Stockholm," Simone said dreamily. "Ask the women about dancing."

She lay back on the pillows. "There's a painting to be unearthed in London from Anna Watridge. Penny Whitewater. Cloe Ricci in Italy. Suzanna Fujimoto. Anya de Jesus, in Barcelona, for dinner...."

Firebrand Books is an award-winning feminist and lesbian publishing house. We are committed to producing quality work in a wide variety of genres by ethnically and racially diverse authors. Now in our fourteenth year, we have over ninety titles in print.

A free catalog is available on request from Firebrand Books, 141 The Commons, Ithaca, New York 14850, 607-272-0000.

Visit our website at www.firebrandbooks.com.